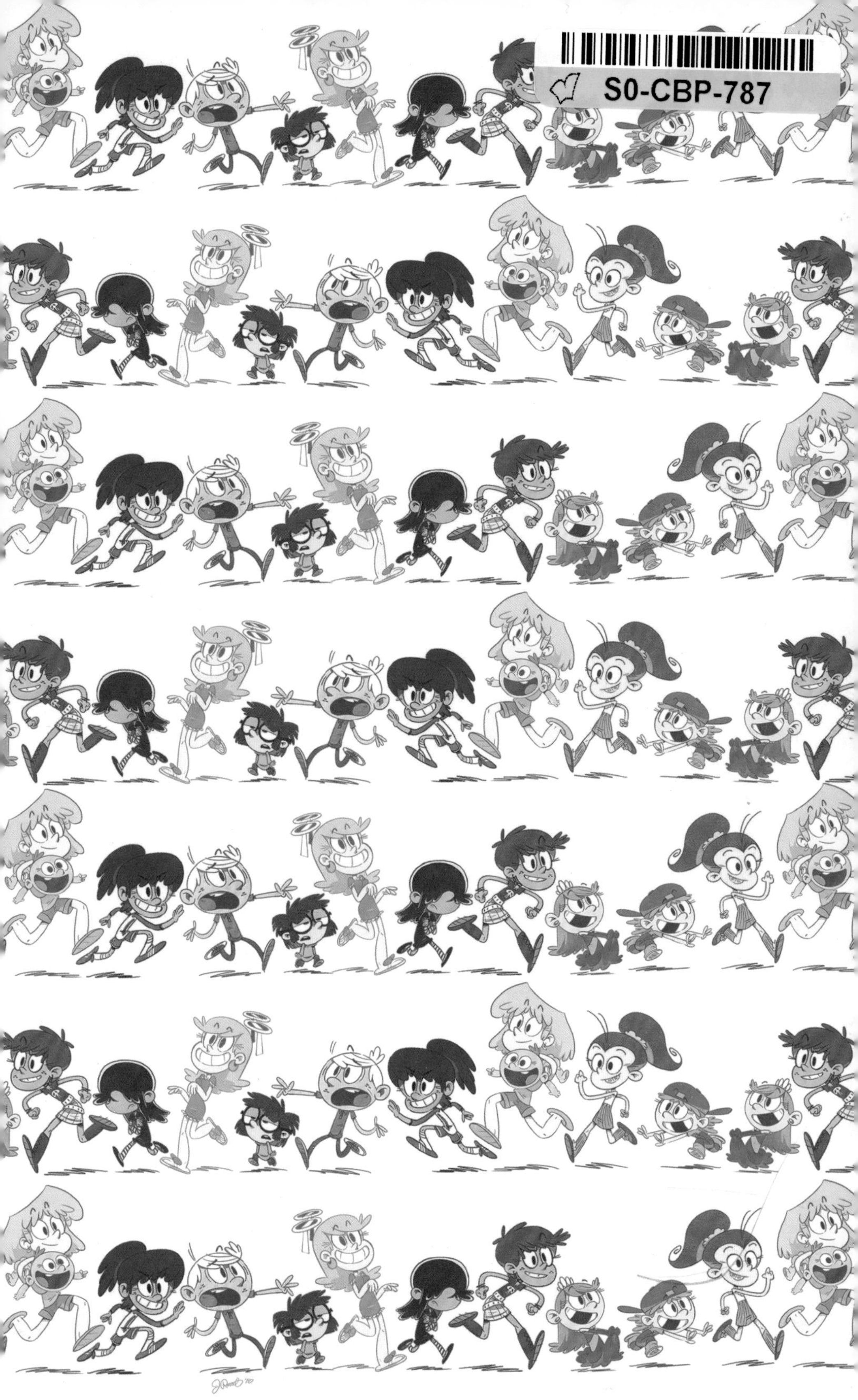

THE LOUD HOUSE

#14 "GUESSING GAMES"

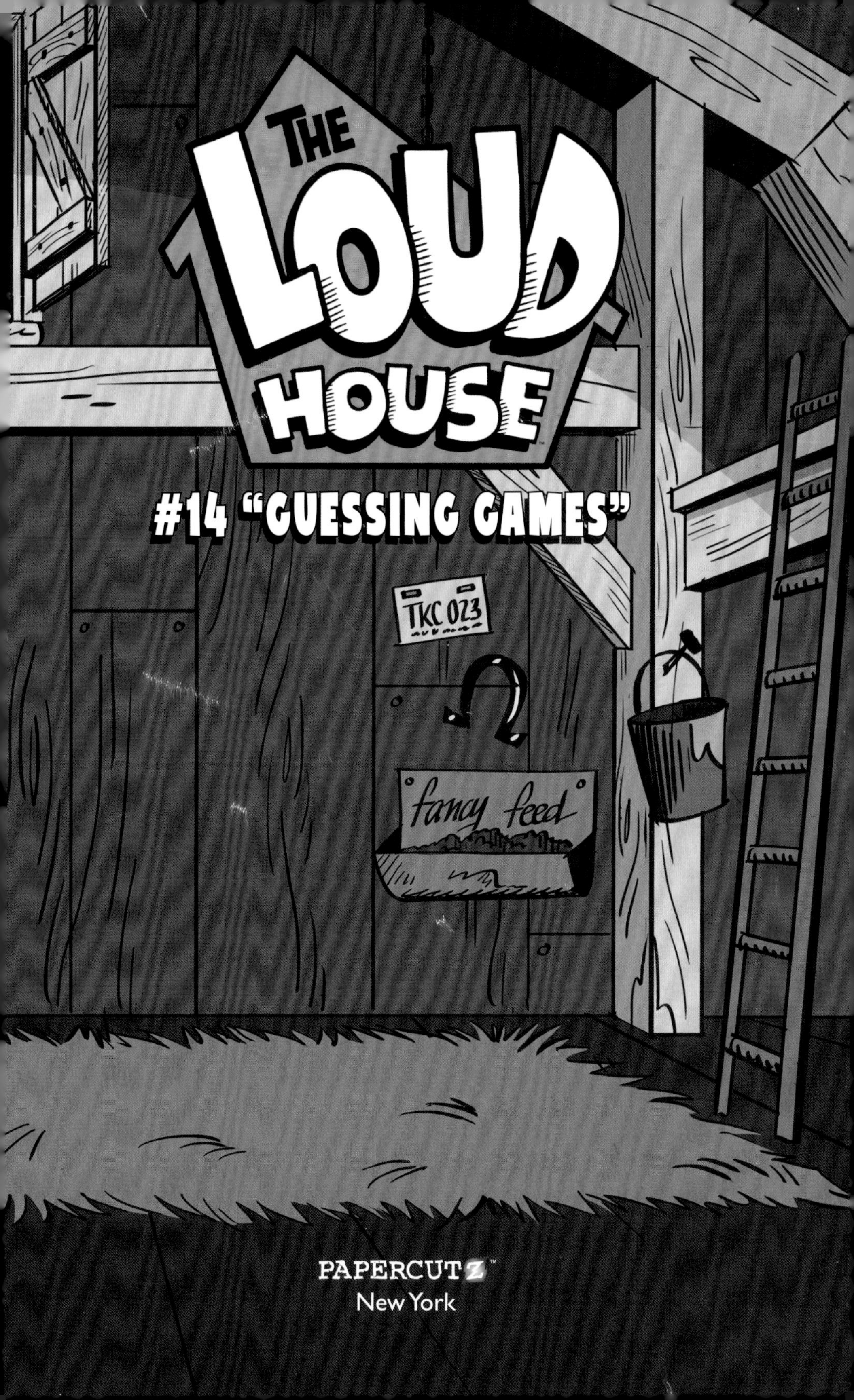
TKC 023
fancy feed

PAPERCUTZ™
New York

nickelodeon GRAPHIC NOVELS AVAILABLE FROM PAPERCUTZ

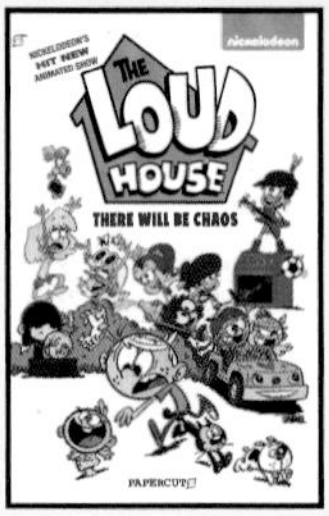
THE LOUD HOUSE
THERE WILL BE CHAOS

THE LOUD HOUSE
#1
"There Will Be Chaos"

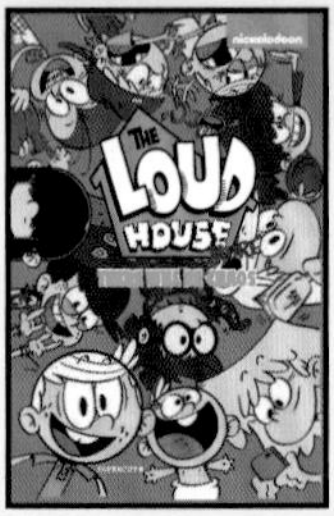
THE LOUD HOUSE

THE LOUD HOUSE
#2
"There Will Be More Chaos"

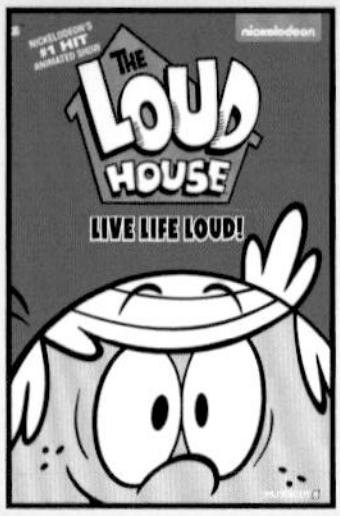
THE LOUD HOUSE
LIVE LIFE LOUD!

THE LOUD HOUSE
#3
"Live Life Loud!"

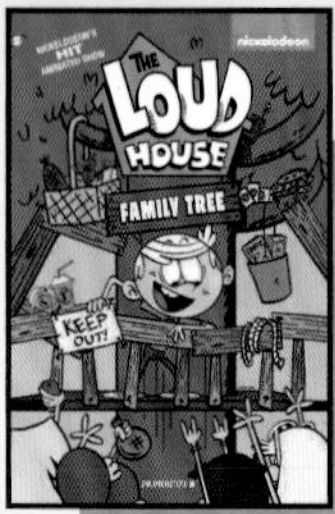
THE LOUD HOUSE
FAMILY TREE
KEEP OUT!

THE LOUD HOUSE
#4
"Family Tree"

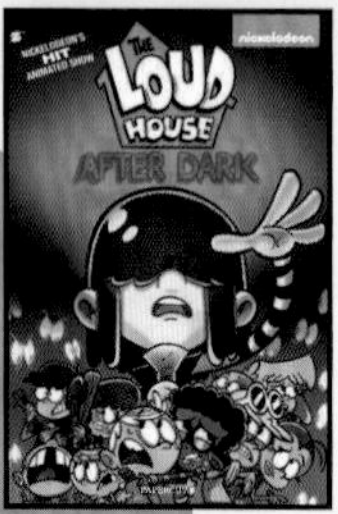
THE LOUD HOUSE
AFTER DARK

THE LOUD HOUSE
#5
"After Dark"

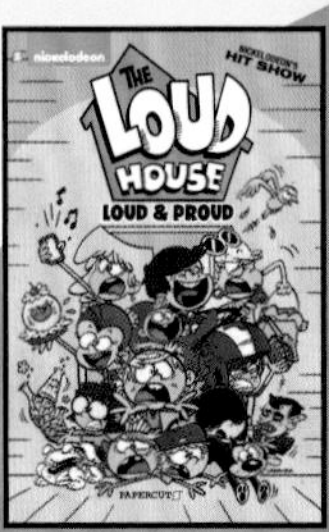
THE LOUD HOUSE
LOUD & PROUD

THE LOUD HOUSE
#6
"Loud and Proud"

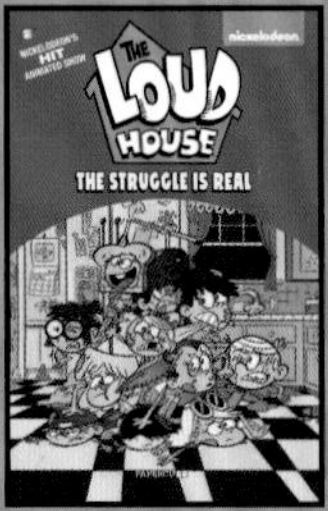
THE LOUD HOUSE
THE STRUGGLE IS REAL

THE LOUD HOUSE
#7
"The Struggle is Real"

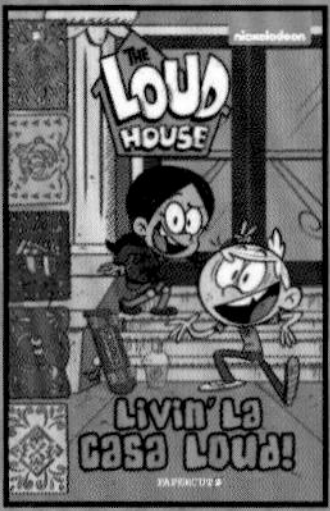
THE LOUD HOUSE
Livin' La Casa Loud!

THE LOUD HOUSE
#8
"Livin' La Casa Loud"

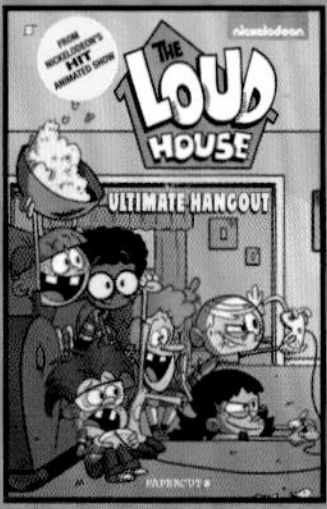
THE LOUD HOUSE
ULTIMATE HANGOUT

THE LOUD HOUSE
#9
"Ultimate Hangout"

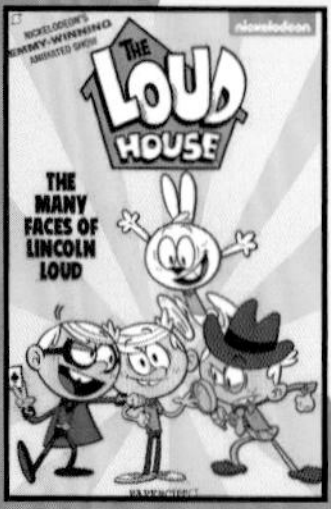
THE LOUD HOUSE
THE MANY FACES OF LINCOLN LOUD

THE LOUD HOUSE
#10
"The Many Faces of Lincoln Loud"

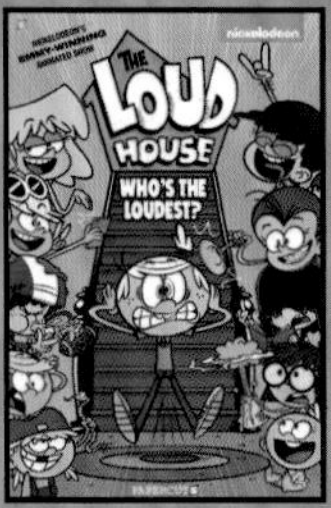
THE LOUD HOUSE
WHO'S THE LOUDEST?

THE LOUD HOUSE
#11
"Who's the Loudest?"

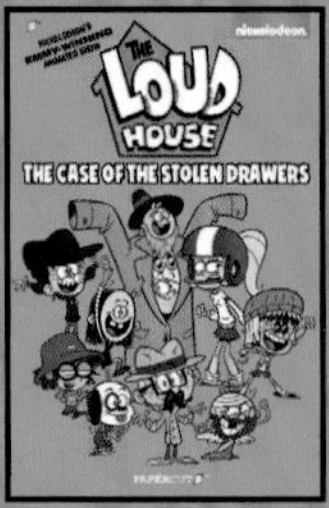
THE LOUD HOUSE
THE CASE OF THE STOLEN DRAWERS

THE LOUD HOUSE
#12
"The Case of the Stolen Drawers"

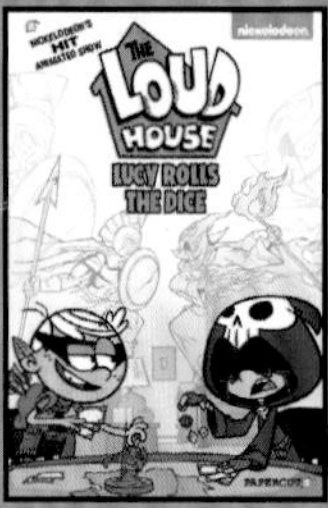
THE LOUD HOUSE
LUCY ROLLS THE DICE

THE LOUD HOUSE
#13
"Lucy Rolls the Dice"

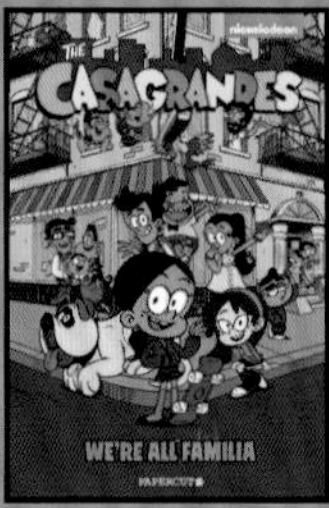
THE CASAGRANDES
WE'RE ALL FAMILIA

THE CASAGRANDES
#1
"We're All Familia"

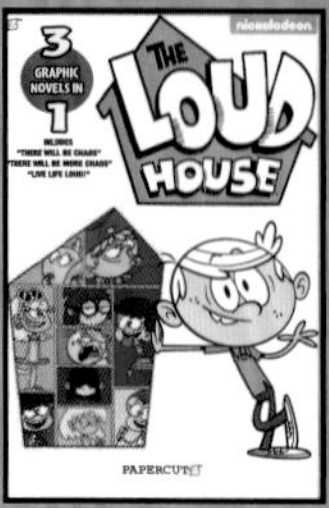
3 GRAPHIC NOVELS IN 1
THE LOUD HOUSE

THE LOUD HOUSE
3 IN 1
#1

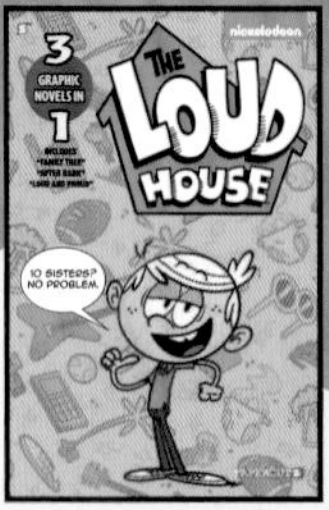
3 GRAPHIC NOVELS IN 1
THE LOUD HOUSE
10 SISTERS? NO PROBLEM.

THE LOUD HOUSE
3 IN 1
#2

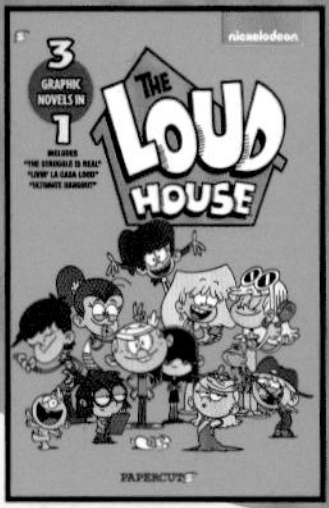
3 GRAPHIC NOVELS IN 1
THE LOUD HOUSE

THE LOUD HOUSE
3 IN 1
#3

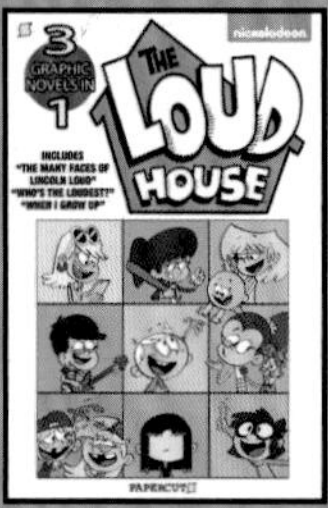
3 GRAPHIC NOVELS IN 1
THE LOUD HOUSE

THE LOUD HOUSE
3 IN 1
#4

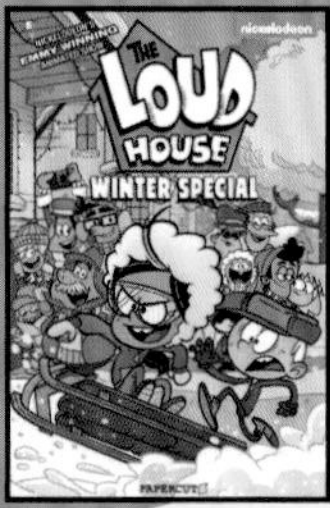
THE LOUD HOUSE
WINTER SPECIAL

THE LOUD HOUSE
WINTER SPECIAL

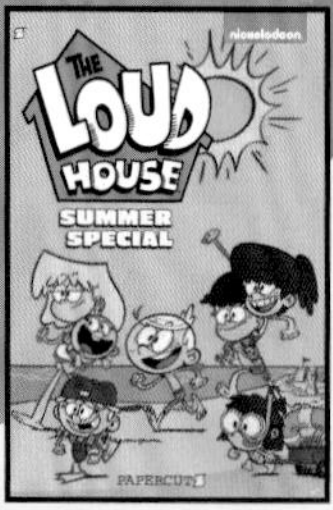
THE LOUD HOUSE
SUMMER SPECIAL

THE LOUD HOUSE
SUMMER SPECIAL

The Loud House graphic novels and specials are available for $7.99 each in paperback, $12.99 each in hardcover. THE LOUD HOUSE 3 IN 1 graphic novels are available for $14.99 each in paperback only.

Available from booksellers everywhere. You can also order online from Papercutz.com, or call 1-800-886-1223, Monday through Friday, 9-5 EST. MC, Visa, and AmEx accepted. To order by mail, please add $5.00 for postage and handling for the first book ordered, $1.00 for each additional book and make check payable to NBM Publishing.
Send to: Papercutz, 160 Broadway, Suite 700, East Wing, New York, NY 10038.

THE LOUD HOUSE

#14 "GUESSING GAMES"

nickelodeon

THE LOUD HOUSE

#14 "GUESSING GAMES"

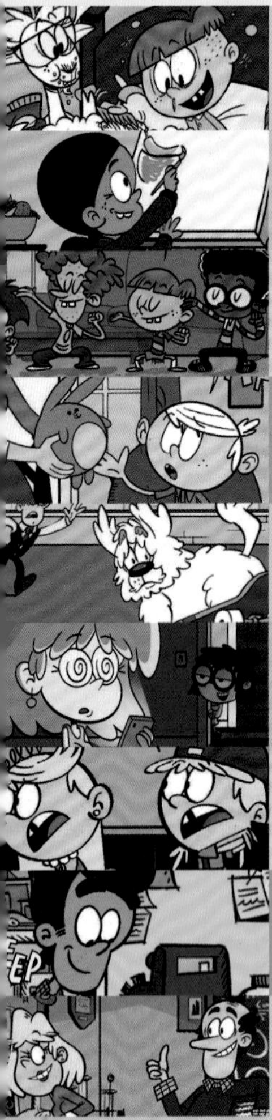

"CRITTER COMFORTS"
Kiernan Sjursen-Lien — Writer
Kelsey Wooley — Artist, Colorist
Wilson Ramos Jr. — Letterer

"GUESS WHO?"
Jair Holguin — Writer
Melissa Kleynowski— Artist
Efrain Rodriguez — Colorist
Wilson Ramos Jr. — Letterer

"TRENDING"
Zamir Ramirez — Writer
Zazo Aguiar — Penciler, Colorist
Karolyne Rocha — Inker
Wilson Ramos Jr. — Letterer

"PROGRAM POSTPONED"
Kiernan Sjursen-Lien — Writer
Angela Zhang — Artist
Efrain Rodriguez — Colorist
Wilson Ramos Jr. — Letterer

"THE GOLDEN BONE"
Kara Fein — Writer
Ron Bradley — Artist, Colorist
Wilson Ramos Jr. — Letterer

"SO SUBLIMINAL"
Kara Fein — Writer
Joel Zamudio— Artist, Colorist
Wilson Ramos Jr. — Letterer

"TICKET FOR TWO"
Kevin Cannarile — Writer
Daniela Rodriguez — Artist, Colorist
Wilson Ramos Jr. — Letterer

"BOBBY'S WORLD "
Jair Holguin — Writer
Amanda Tran — Artist, Colorist
Wilson Ramos Jr. — Letterer

"ON THE HUSH HUSH"
Whitney Wetta — Writer
Zazo Aguiar — Artist, Colorist
Wilson Ramos Jr. — Letterer

"COUNTRY MOUSE,
SUBURBAN HAMSTER"
Kacey Wooley-Huang — Writer
Kelsey Wooley — Artist, Colorist
Wilson Ramos Jr. — Letterer

"WALKMAN THE LINE"
Caitlin Fein — Writer
Max Alley — Artist
Joel Zamudio — Colorist
Wilson Ramos Jr. — Letterer

"SINGING OUT LOUD"
Kacey Wooley-Huang — Writer
Amanda Lioi — Artist, Colorist
Wilson Ramos Jr. — Letterer

"10 SECONDS TO PERFECT"
Kara Fein — Writer
Jose Hernandez — Artist, Colorist
Wilson Ramos Jr. — Letterer

TWINTUITION"
Caitlin Fein — Writer
Melissa Kleynowski — Artist
Peter Bertucci — Colorist
Wilson Ramos Jr. — Letterer

"FURIENDLY COMPETITION"
Kiernan Sjursen-Lien — Writer
DK Terrell — Artist, Colorist
Wilson Ramos Jr. — Letterer

"BUGGIN' OUT"
Zamir Ramirez — Writer
Joel Zamudio — Artist, Colorist
Wilson Ramos Jr. — Letterer

"SALE FAIL"
Caitlin Fein— Writer
Max Alley — Artist,
Joel Zamudio — Colorist
Wilson Ramos Jr. — Letterer

KELSEY WOOLEY — Cover Artist

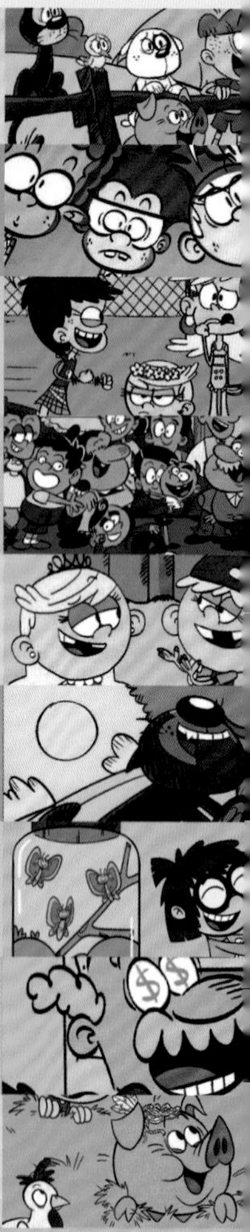

JORDAN ROSATO — Endpapers
JAMES SALERNO — Sr. Art Director/Nickelodeon
JAYJAY JACKSON — Design
EMMA BONE, CAITLIN FEIN, KRISTEN G. SMITH, NEIL WADE, DANA CLUVERIUS, MOLLIE FREILICH — Special Thanks
JORDAN HILLMAN — Editorial Intern
JEFF WHITMAN — Editor
JOAN HILTY — Editor/Nickelodeon
JIM SALICRUP
Editor-in-Chief

ISBN: 978-1-5458-0724-8 paperback edition
ISBN: 978-1-5458-0723-1 hardcover edition

www.papercutz.com

Papercutz books may be purchased for business or promotional use. For information on bulk purchases please contact Macmillan Corporate and Premium Sales Department at (800) 221-7945 x5442.

Printed in China
December 2021

Distributed by Macmillan
First Printing

MEET THE LOUD FAMILY
and friends!

LINCOLN LOUD
THE MIDDLE CHILD

Lincoln is the middle child, with five older sisters and five younger sisters. He has learned that surviving the Loud household means staying a step ahead. He's the man with a plan, always coming up with a way to get what he wants or deal with a problem, even if things inevitably go wrong. Being the only boy comes with some perks. Lincoln gets his own room – even if it's just a converted linen closet. On the other hand, being the only boy also means he sometimes gets a little too much attention from his sisters. They mother him, tease him, and use him as the occasional lab rat or fashion show participant. Lincoln's sisters may drive him crazy, but he loves them and is always willing to help out if they need him.

LORI LOUD
THE OLDEST

As the first-born child of the Loud Clan, Lori sees herself as the boss of all her siblings. She feels she's paved the way for them and deserves extra respect. Her signature traits are rolling her eyes, texting her boyfriend, Bobby, and literally saying "literally" all the time. Because she's the oldest and most experienced sibling, Lori can be a great ally, so it pays to stay on her good side, especially since she can drive.

LENI LOUD
THE FASHIONISTA

Leni spends most of her time designing outfits and accessorizing. She always falls for Luan's pranks, and sometimes walks into walls when she's talking (she's not great at doing two things at once). Leni might be flighty, but she's the sweetest of the Loud siblings and truly has a heart of gold (even though she's pretty sure it's a heart of blood).

LUNA LOUD
THE ROCK STAR

Luna is loud, boisterous, freewheeling, and her energy is always cranked to 11. She thinks about music so much that she even talks in song lyrics. On the off-chance she doesn't have her guitar with her, everything can and will be turned into a musical instrument. You can always count on Luna to help out, and she'll do most anything you ask, as long as you're okay with her supplying a rocking guitar accompaniment.

LUAN LOUD
THE JOKESTER

Luan's a standup comedienne who provides a non-stop barrage of silly puns. She's big on prop comedy too – squirting flowers and whoopee cushions – so you have to be on your toes whenever she's around. She loves to pull pranks and is a really good ventriloquist – she is often found doing bits with her dummy, Mr. Coconuts. Luan never lets anything get her down; to her, laughter IS the best medicine.

LYNN LOUD
THE ATHLETE

Lynn is athletic and full of energy and is always looking for a teammate. With her, it's all sports all the time. She'll turn anything into a sport. Putting away eggs? Jump shot! Score! Cleaning up the eggs? Slap shot! Score! Lynn is very competitive, but despite her competitive nature, she always tries to just have a good time.

LUCY LOUD
THE EMO

You can always count on Lucy to give the morbid point of view in any given situation. She is obsessed with all things spooky and dark – funerals, vampires, séances, and the like. She wears mostly black and writes moody poetry. She's usually quiet and keeps to herself. Lucy has a way of mysteriously appearing out of nowhere, and try as they might, her siblings never get used to this.

LOLA LOUD
THE BEAUTY QUEEN)

Lola could not be more different from her twin sister, Lana. She's a pageant powerhouse whose interests include glitter, photo shoots, and her own beautiful, beautiful face. But don't let her cute, gap-toothed smile fool you; underneath all the sugar and spice lurks a Machiavellian mastermind. Whatever Lola wants, Lola gets – or else. She's the eyes and ears of the household and never resists an opportunity to tattle on troublemakers. But if you stay on Lola's good side, you've got yourself a fierce ally – and a lifetime supply of free makeovers.

LANA LOUD
THE TOMBOY

Lana is the rough-and-tumble sparkplug counterpart to her twin sister, Lola. She's all about reptiles, mud pies, and muffler repair. She's the resident Ms. Fix-it and is always ready to lend a hand – the dirtier the job, the better. Need your toilet unclogged? Snake fed? Back-zit popped? Lana's your gal. All she asks in return is a little A-B-C gum, or a handful of kibble (she often sneaks it from the dog bowl).

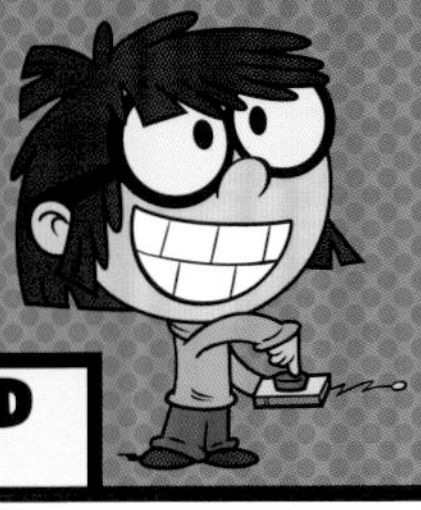

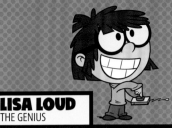

LISA LOUD
THE GENIUS

Lisa is smarter than the rest of her siblings combined. She'll most likely be a rocket scientist, or a brain surgeon, or an evil genius who takes over the world. Lisa spends most of her time working in her lab (the family has gotten used to the explosions), and says her research leaves little time for frivolous human pursuits like "playing" or "getting haircuts." That said, she's always there to help with a homework question, or to explain why the sky is blue, or to point out the structural flaws in someone's pillow fort. Lisa says it's the least she can do for her favorite test subjects, er, siblings.

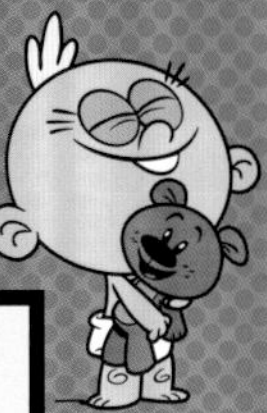

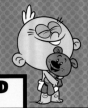

LILY LOUD
THE BABY

Lily is a giggly, drooly, diaper-ditching free spirit, affectionately known as "the poop machine." You can't keep a nappy on this kid – she's like a teething Houdini. But even when Lily's running wild, dropping rancid diaper bombs, or drooling all over the remote, she always brings a smile to everyone's face (and a clothespin to their nose). Lily is everyone's favorite little buddy, and the whole family loves her unconditionally.

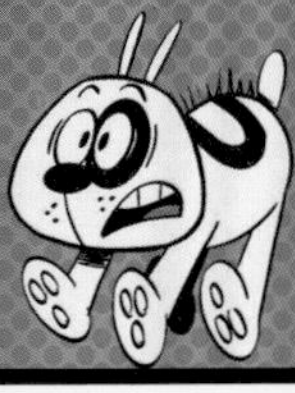

CHARLES

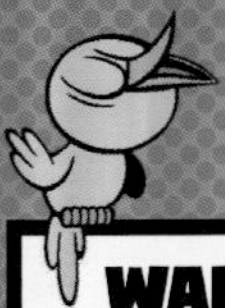

WALT

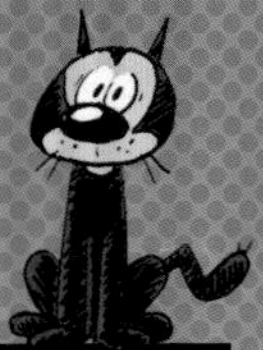

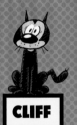

CLIFF

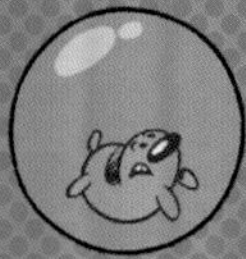

GEO

RITA LOUD

Mother to the eleven Loud kids, Mom (Rita Loud) wears many different hats. She's a chauffeur, homework-checker and barf-cleaner-upper all rolled into one. She's always there for her kids and ready to jump into action during a crisis, whether it's a fight between the twins or Leni's missing shoe. When she's not chasing the kids around or at her day job as a dental hygienist, Mom pursues her passion: writing. She also loves taking on house projects and is very handy with tools (guess that's where Lana gets it from). Between writing, working and being a mom, her days are always hectic but she wouldn't have it any other way.

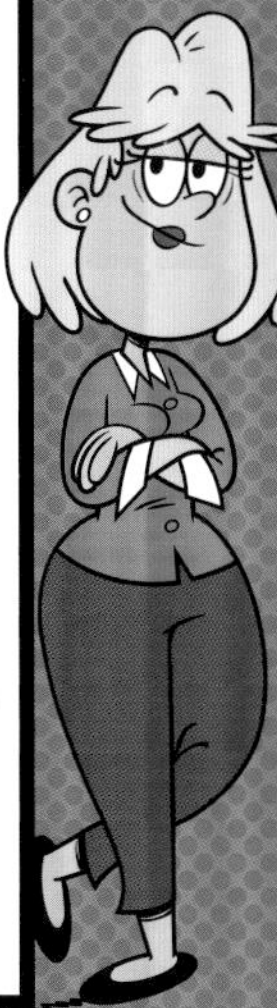

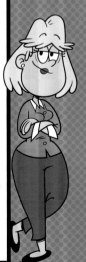

LYNN LOUD SR.

Dad (Lynn Loud Sr.) is a fun-loving, upbeat aspiring chef. A kid-at-heart, he's not above taking part in the kids' zany schemes. In addition to cooking, Dad loves his van, playing the cowbell and making puns. Before meeting Mom, Dad spent a semester in England and has been obsessed with British culture ever since – and sometimes "accidentally" slips into a British accent. When Dad's not wrangling the kids, he's pursuing his dream of opening his own restaurant where he hopes to make his "Lynn-sagnas" world-famous.

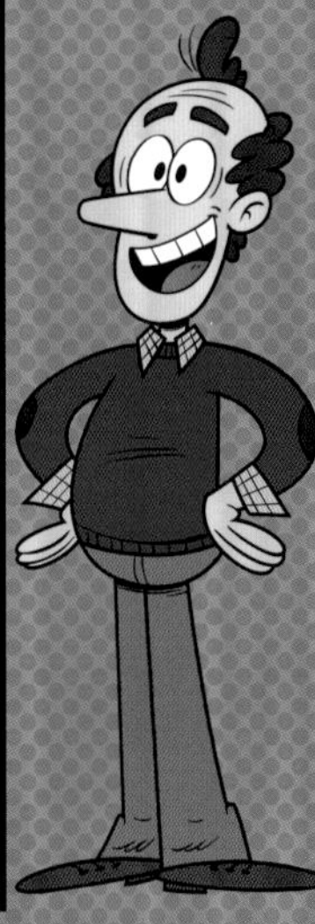

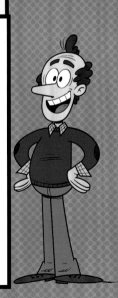

RUSTY SPOKES

Rusty is a self-proclaimed ladies' man who's always the first to dish out girl advice—even though he's never been on an actual date. His dad owns a suit rental service, so occasionally Rusty can hook the gang up with some dapper duds—just as long as no one gets anything dirty.

ZACH GURDLE

Zach is a self-admitted nerd who's obsessed with aliens and conspiracy theories. He lives between a freeway and a circus, so the chaos of the Loud House doesn't faze him. He and Rusty occasionally butt heads, but deep down, it's all love.

STELLA

Stella, is a quirky, carefree girl who's new to Royal Woods. She has tons of interests, like trying on wigs, playing laser tag, eating curly fries, and hanging with her friends. But what she loves the most is tech — she always wants to dismantle electronics and put them back together again.

LIAM

Liam is an enthusiastic, sweet-natured farm boy full of down-home wisdom. He loves hanging out with his Mee Maw, wrestling his prize pig Virginia, and sharing his farm-to-table produce with the rest of the gang.

VIRGINIA

FLIP

The owner of Flip's Food & Fuel, the local convenience store. Flip has questionable business practices — he's been known to sell expired milk and stick his feet in the nacho cheese! When he's not selling Flippees, Flip loves fishing and also sponsors Lynn's rec basketball team.

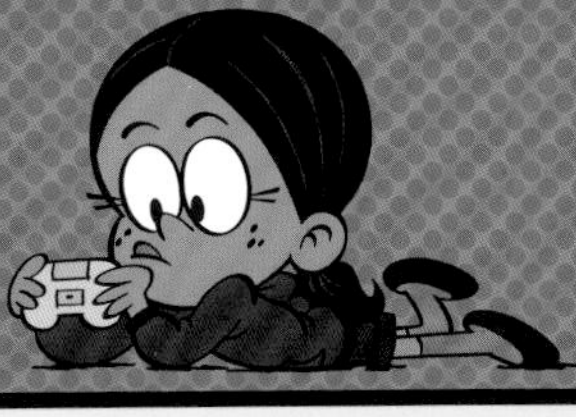

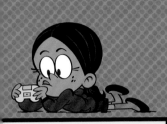

RONNIE ANNE SANTIAGO

Ronnie Anne's a skateboarding city girl now. She's fearless, free-spirited, and always quick to come up with a plan. She's one tough cookie, but she also has a sweet side. Ronnie Anne loves helping her family, and that's taught her to help others, too. When she's not pitching in at the family mercado, you can find her exploring the neighborhood with her best friend Sid, or ordering hot dogs with her skater buds Casey, Nikki, and Sameer.

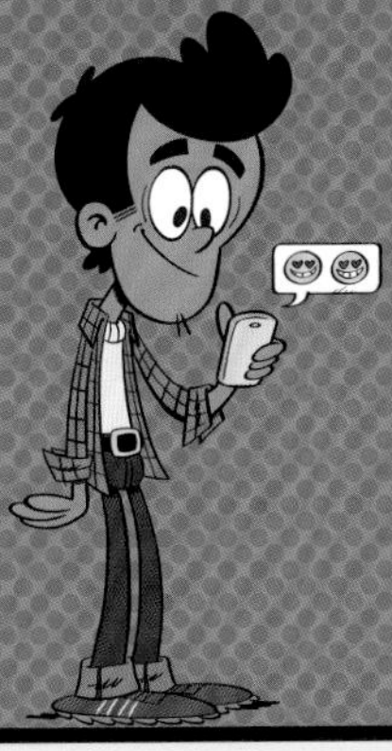

BOBBY SANTIAGO

Bobby is Ronnie Anne's big bro. He's a student and one of the hardest workers in the city! He loves his family and loves working at the Mercado. As his Abuelo's right hand man, Bobby can't wait to take over the family business one day. He's a big kid at heart, and his clumsiness gets him into some sticky situations at work, like locking himself in the freezer. Mercado mishaps aside, everyone in the neighborhood loves to come to the store and talk to Bobby.

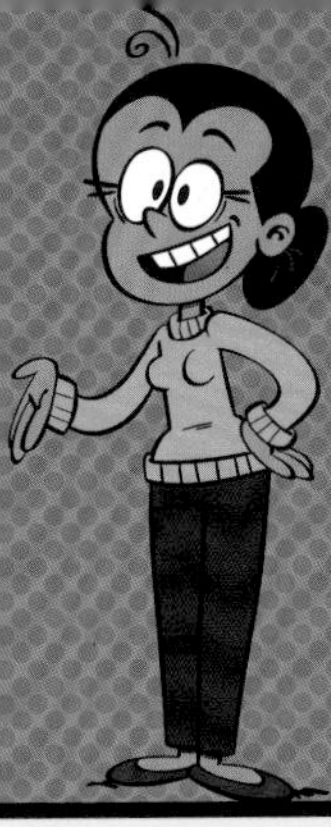

MARIA CASAGRANDE SANTIAGO

She's the mother of Bobby and Ronnie Anne. A hardworking nurse, she doesn't get to spend a lot of time with her kids, but when she does she treasures it. Maria is calm and rational but often worries about whether she's doing enough for her kids. Maria, Bobby, and Ronnie Anne are a close-knit trio who were used to having only each other – until they moved in with their extended family.

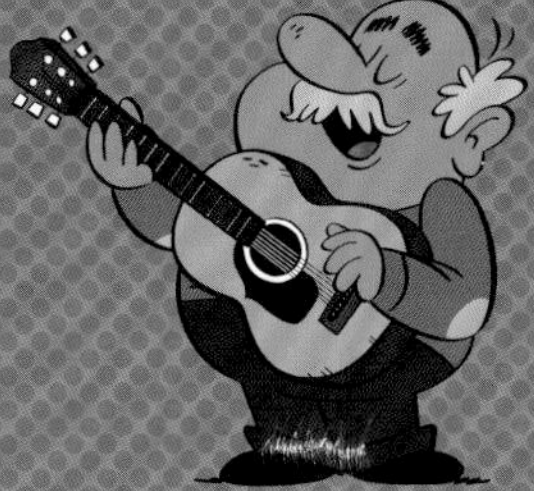

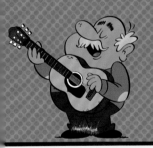

HECTOR CASAGRANDE

Hector is Carlos and Maria's dad, and the Abuelo of the family (that means grandpa)! He owns the Mercado on the ground floor of their apartment building and takes great pride in his work, his family, and being the unofficial "mayor" of the block. He loves to tell stories, share his ideas, and gossip (even though he won't admit to it). You can find him working in the Mercado, playing guitar, or watching his favorite telenovela.

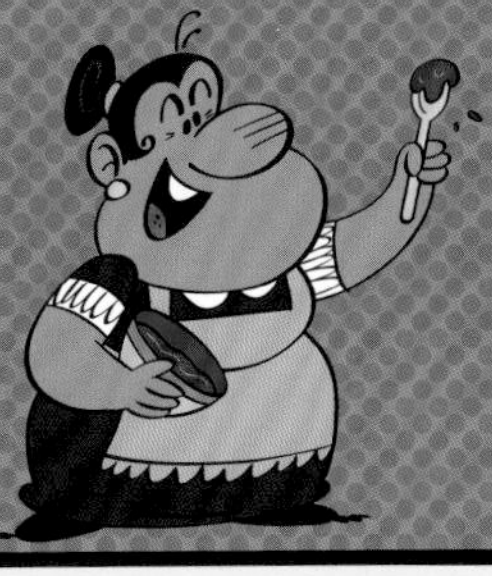

ROSA CASAGRANDE

Rosa is Carlos and Maria's mom and the Abuela of the family (that means grandma)! She's the head of the household, the wisest Casagrande, and the master cook with a superhuman ability to tell when anyone in the house is hungry. She often tries to fix problems or illnesses with traditional Mexican home remedies and potions. She's very protective of her family… sometimes a little too much.

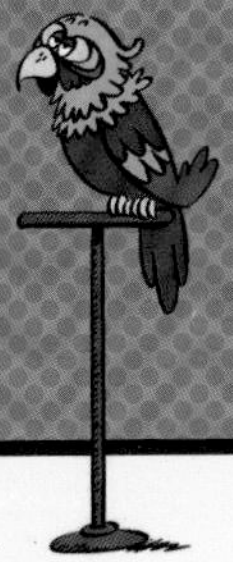

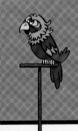

SERGIO

Sergio is the Casagrandes' beloved pet parrot. He's a blunt, sassy bird who "thinks" he's full of wisdom, and always has something to say. The Casagrandes have to keep a close eye on their credit card as Sergio is addicted to online shopping and is always asking the family to buy him some new gadget he saw on TV. Sergio is most loyal to Rosa and serves as her wing-man, partner in crime, taste tester, and confidant. Sergio is quite popular in the neighborhood and is always up for a good time.

CARLOS CASAGRANDE

Carlos is Maria's brother. He's married to Frida, and together they have four kids: Carlota, C.J., Carl, and Carlitos. Carlos is a Professor of Cultural Studies at a local college. Usually he has his heads in the clouds or his nose in a textbook. Relatively easygoing, Carlos is a loving father and an enthusiastic teacher who tries to get his kids interested in their Mexican heritage.

FRIDA PUGA CASAGRANDE

Frida is Carlos, C.J., Carl, and Carlitos' mom. She's an art professor and a performance artist, and is always looking for new ways to express herself. She's got a big heart and isn't shy about her emotions. Frida tends to cry when she's sad, happy, angry, or any other emotion you can think of. She's always up for fun, is passionate about her art, and loves her family more than anything.

CARLOTA CASAGRANDE

Carlota is CJ, Carl, and Carlitos' older sister. A social media influencer, she's excited to be like a big sister to Ronnie Anne. She's a force to be reckoned with, and is always trying to share her distinctive vintage style tips with Ronnie Anne.

CARLITOS CASAGRANDE

Carlitos is the baby of the family, and is always copying the behavior of everyone in the household—even if they aren't human. He's a playful and silly baby who loves to play with the family pets.

CJ (CARLOS JR.) CASAGRANDE

CJ is Carlota's younger brother and Carl and Carlitos' older brother. He was born with Down Syndrome. He lights up any room with his infectious smile and is always ready to play. He's obsessed with pirates and is BFFs with Bobby. He likes to wear a bowtie to any family occasion, and you can always catch him laughing or helping his *abuela*.

CARL CASAGRANDE

Carl is wise beyond his years. He's confident, outgoing, and puts a lot of time and effort into looking good. He likes to think of himself as a suave businessman and doesn't like to get caught playing with his action figures or wearing his footie PJs. Even though Bobby is nothing but nice to him, Carl sees his big cousin as his biggest rival.

LALO

Lalo is a slobbery bull mastiff who thinks he's a lapdog. He's not the smartest pup, and gets scared easily… but he loves his family and loves to cuddle.

"CRITTER COMFORTS"

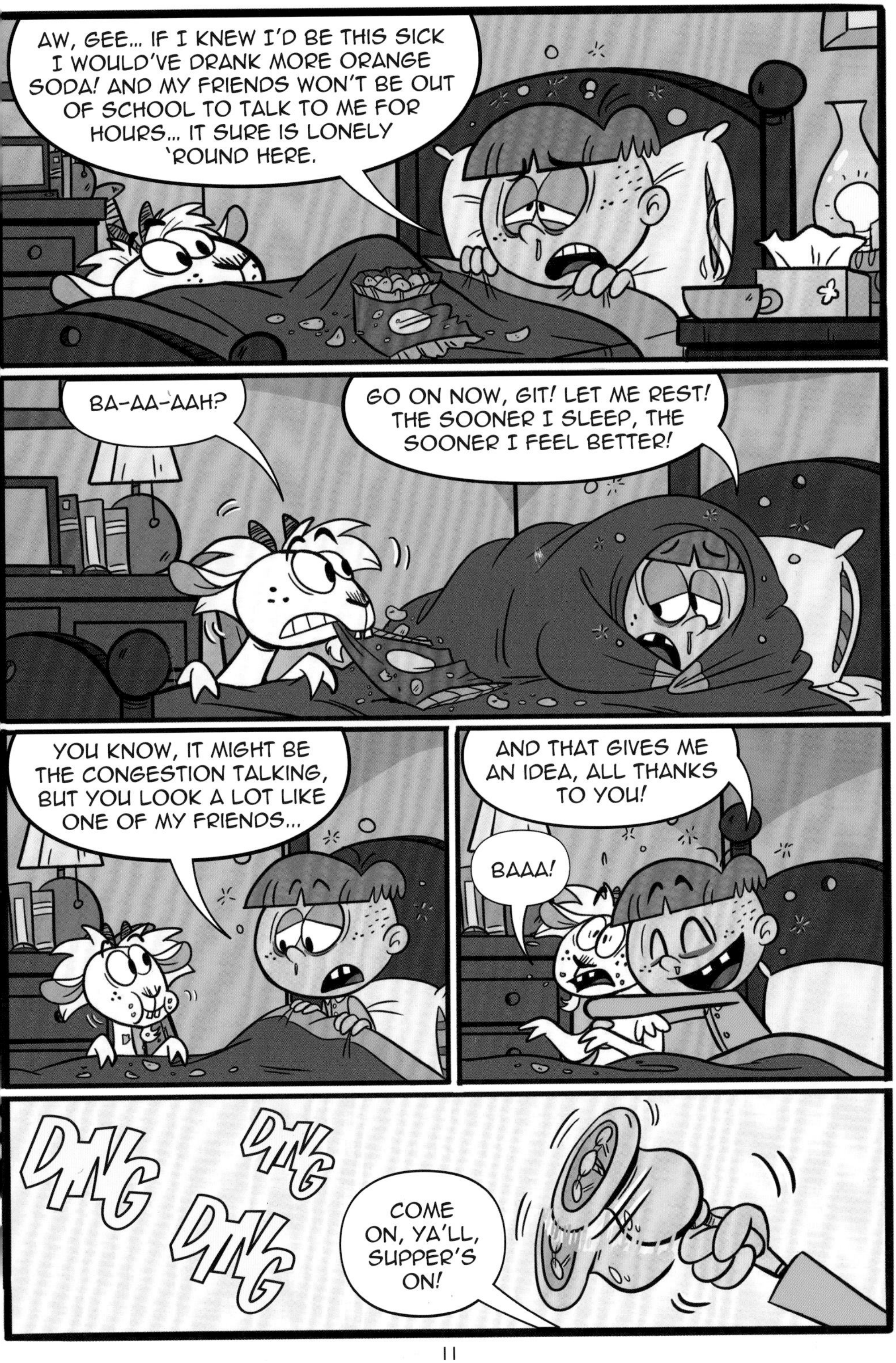
AW, GEE... IF I KNEW I'D BE THIS SICK I WOULD'VE DRANK MORE ORANGE SODA! AND MY FRIENDS WON'T BE OUT OF SCHOOL TO TALK TO ME FOR HOURS... IT SURE IS LONELY 'ROUND HERE.
BA-AA-AAH?
GO ON NOW, GIT! LET ME REST! THE SOONER I SLEEP, THE SOONER I FEEL BETTER!
YOU KNOW, IT MIGHT BE THE CONGESTION TALKING, BUT YOU LOOK A LOT LIKE ONE OF MY FRIENDS...
AND THAT GIVES ME AN IDEA, ALL THANKS TO YOU!
BAAA!
DING
DING
DING
COME ON, YA'LL, SUPPER'S ON!

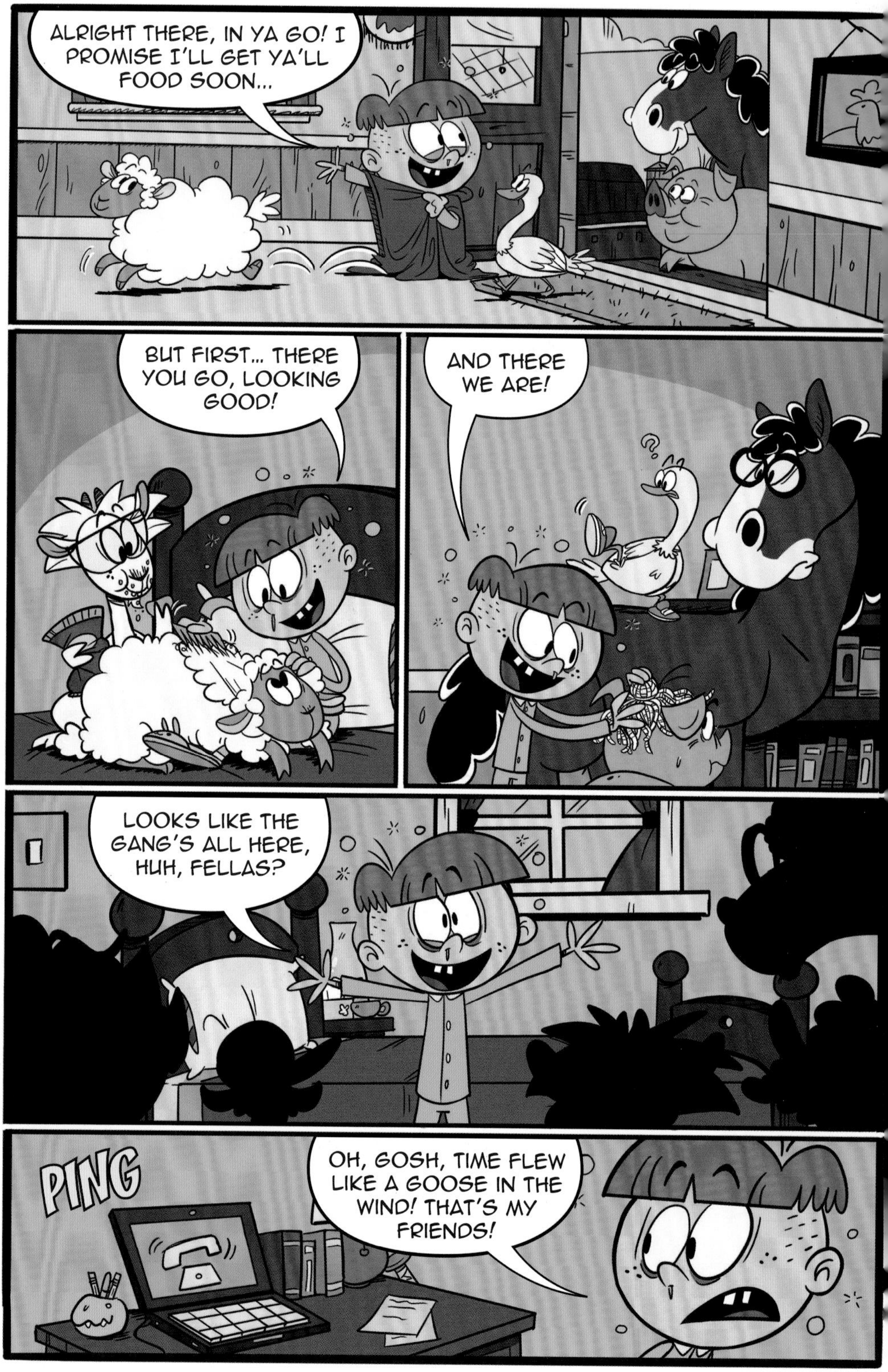
ALRIGHT THERE, IN YA GO! I PROMISE I'LL GET YA'LL FOOD SOON...
BUT FIRST... THERE YOU GO, LOOKING GOOD!
AND THERE WE ARE!
LOOKS LIKE THE GANG'S ALL HERE, HUH, FELLAS?
PING
OH, GOSH, TIME FLEW LIKE A GOOSE IN THE WIND! THAT'S MY FRIENDS!

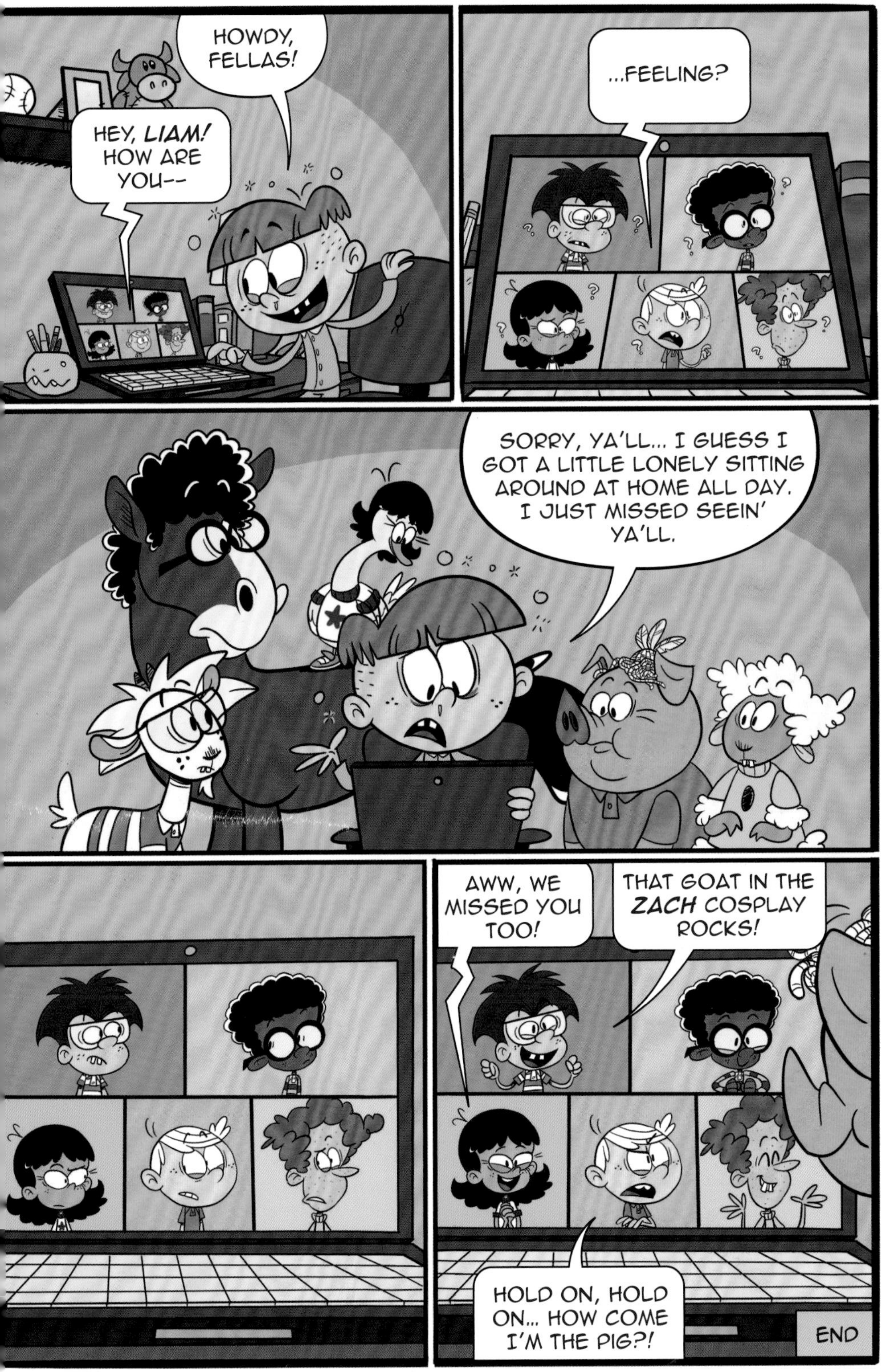
HOWDY, FELLAS!
HEY, LIAM! HOW ARE YOU--
...FEELING?
SORRY, YA'LL... I GUESS I GOT A LITTLE LONELY SITTING AROUND AT HOME ALL DAY. I JUST MISSED SEEIN' YA'LL.
AWW, WE MISSED YOU TOO!
THAT GOAT IN THE ZACH COSPLAY ROCKS!
HOLD ON, HOLD ON... HOW COME I'M THE PIG?!
END

"GUESS WHO"

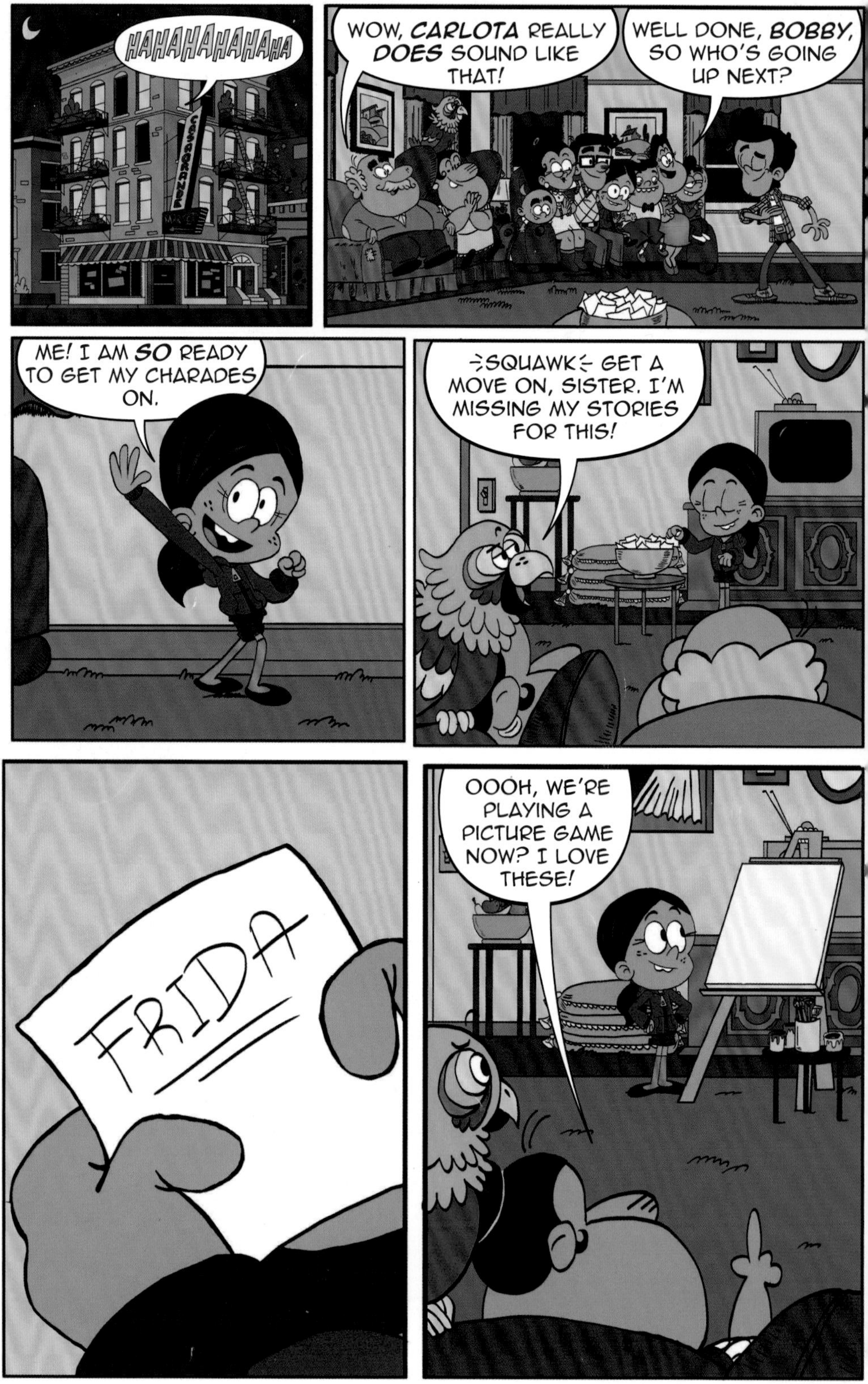

HAHAHAHAHAHAHA
CASAGRANDE
WOW, CARLOTA REALLY DOES SOUND LIKE THAT!
WELL DONE, BOBBY, SO WHO'S GOING UP NEXT?
ME! I AM SO READY TO GET MY CHARADES ON.
SQUAWK GET A MOVE ON, SISTER. I'M MISSING MY STORIES FOR THIS!
FRIDA
OOOH, WE'RE PLAYING A PICTURE GAME NOW? I LOVE THESE!

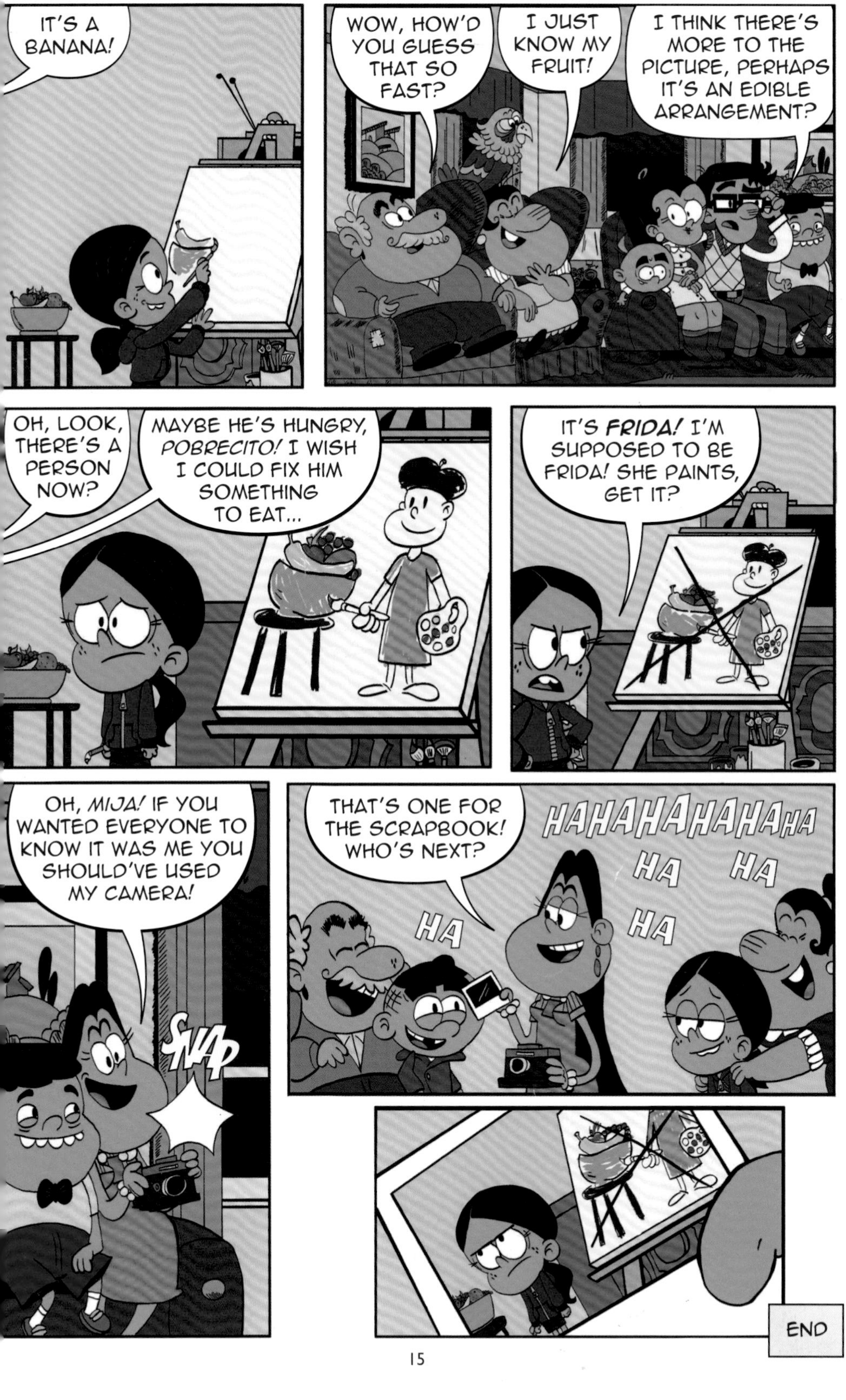

IT'S A BANANA!
WOW, HOW'D YOU GUESS THAT SO FAST?
I JUST KNOW MY FRUIT!
I THINK THERE'S MORE TO THE PICTURE, PERHAPS IT'S AN EDIBLE ARRANGEMENT?
OH, LOOK, THERE'S A PERSON NOW?
MAYBE HE'S HUNGRY, *POBRECITO!* I WISH I COULD FIX HIM SOMETHING TO EAT...
IT'S ***FRIDA!*** I'M SUPPOSED TO BE FRIDA! SHE PAINTS, GET IT?
OH, *MIJA!* IF YOU WANTED EVERYONE TO KNOW IT WAS ME YOU SHOULD'VE USED MY CAMERA!
SNAP
THAT'S ONE FOR THE SCRAPBOOK! WHO'S NEXT?
HAHAHAHAHAHAHA
HA
HA
HA
HA
END

"TRENDING"

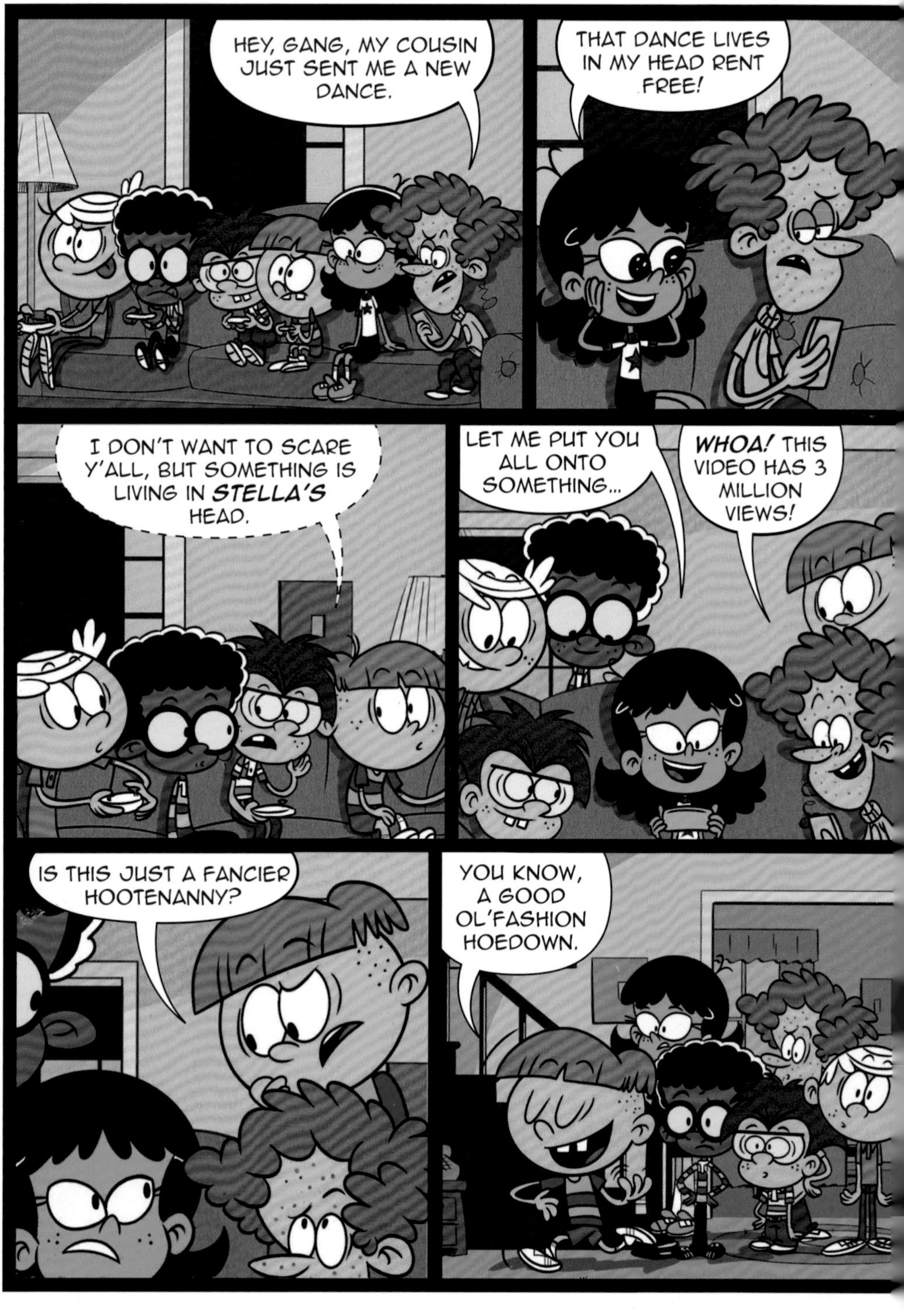

HEY, GANG, MY COUSIN JUST SENT ME A NEW DANCE.
THAT DANCE LIVES IN MY HEAD RENT FREE!
I DON'T WANT TO SCARE Y'ALL, BUT SOMETHING IS LIVING IN STELLA'S HEAD.
LET ME PUT YOU ALL ONTO SOMETHING...
WHOA! THIS VIDEO HAS 3 MILLION VIEWS!
IS THIS JUST A FANCIER HOOTENANNY?
YOU KNOW, A GOOD OL'FASHION HOEDOWN.

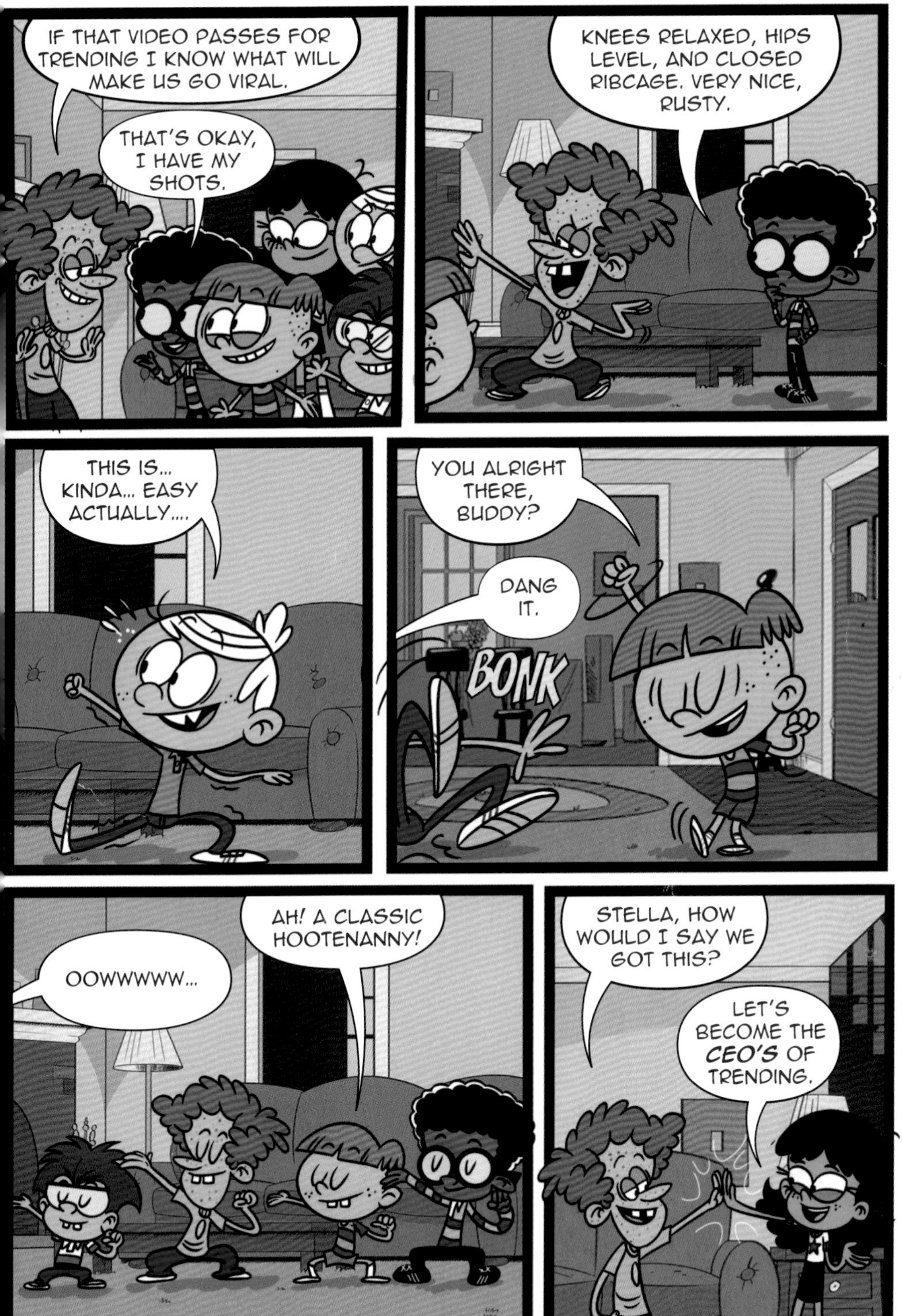
IF THAT VIDEO PASSES FOR TRENDING I KNOW WHAT WILL MAKE US GO VIRAL.
THAT'S OKAY, I HAVE MY SHOTS.
KNEES RELAXED, HIPS LEVEL, AND CLOSED RIBCAGE. VERY NICE, RUSTY.
THIS IS... KINDA... EASY ACTUALLY....
YOU ALRIGHT THERE, BUDDY?
DANG IT.
BONK
OOWWWWW...
AH! A CLASSIC HOOTENANNY!
STELLA, HOW WOULD I SAY WE GOT THIS?
LET'S BECOME THE *CEO'S* OF TRENDING.

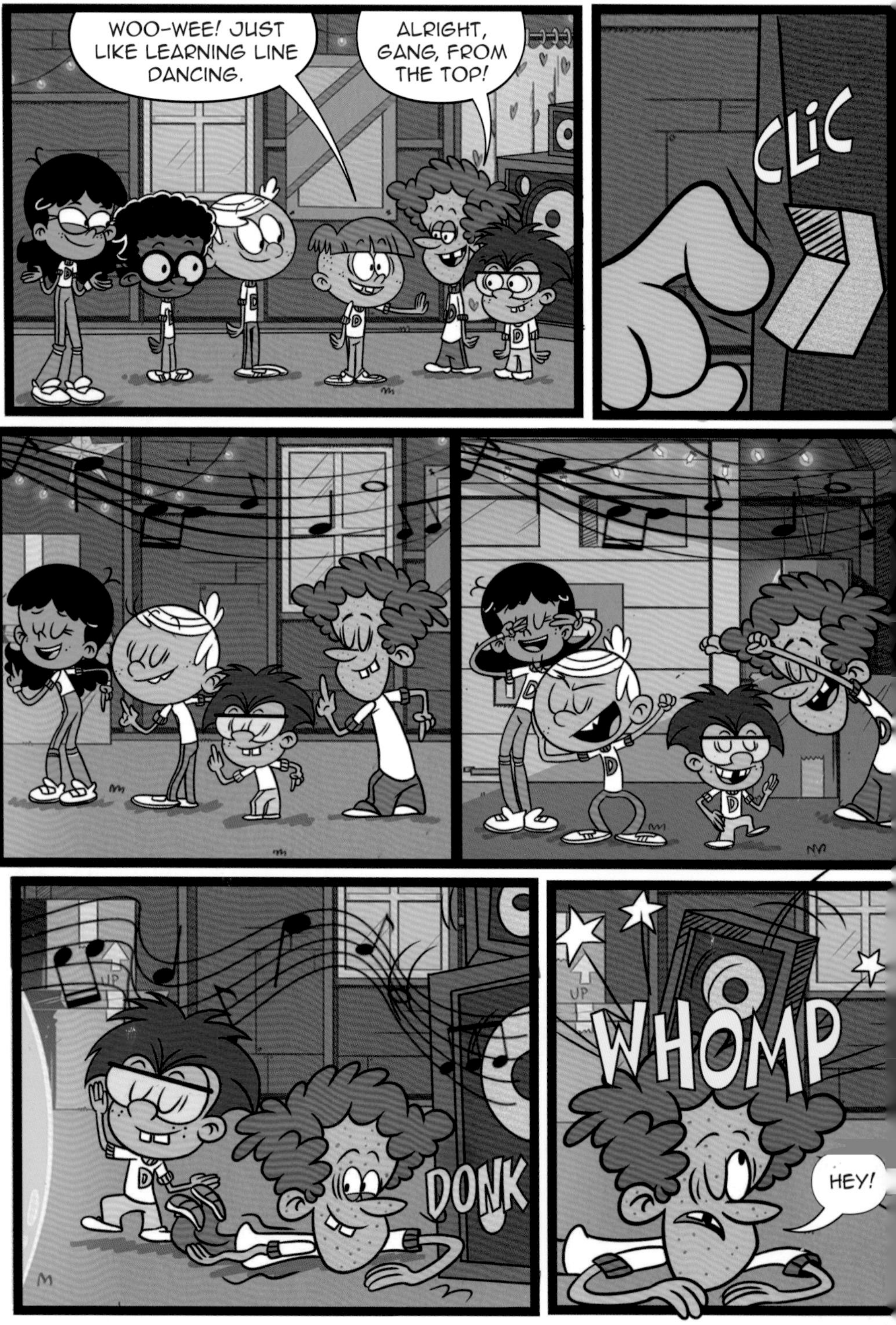

WOO-WEE! JUST LIKE LEARNING LINE DANCING.
ALRIGHT, GANG, FROM THE TOP!
CLIC
DONK
WHOMP
HEY!

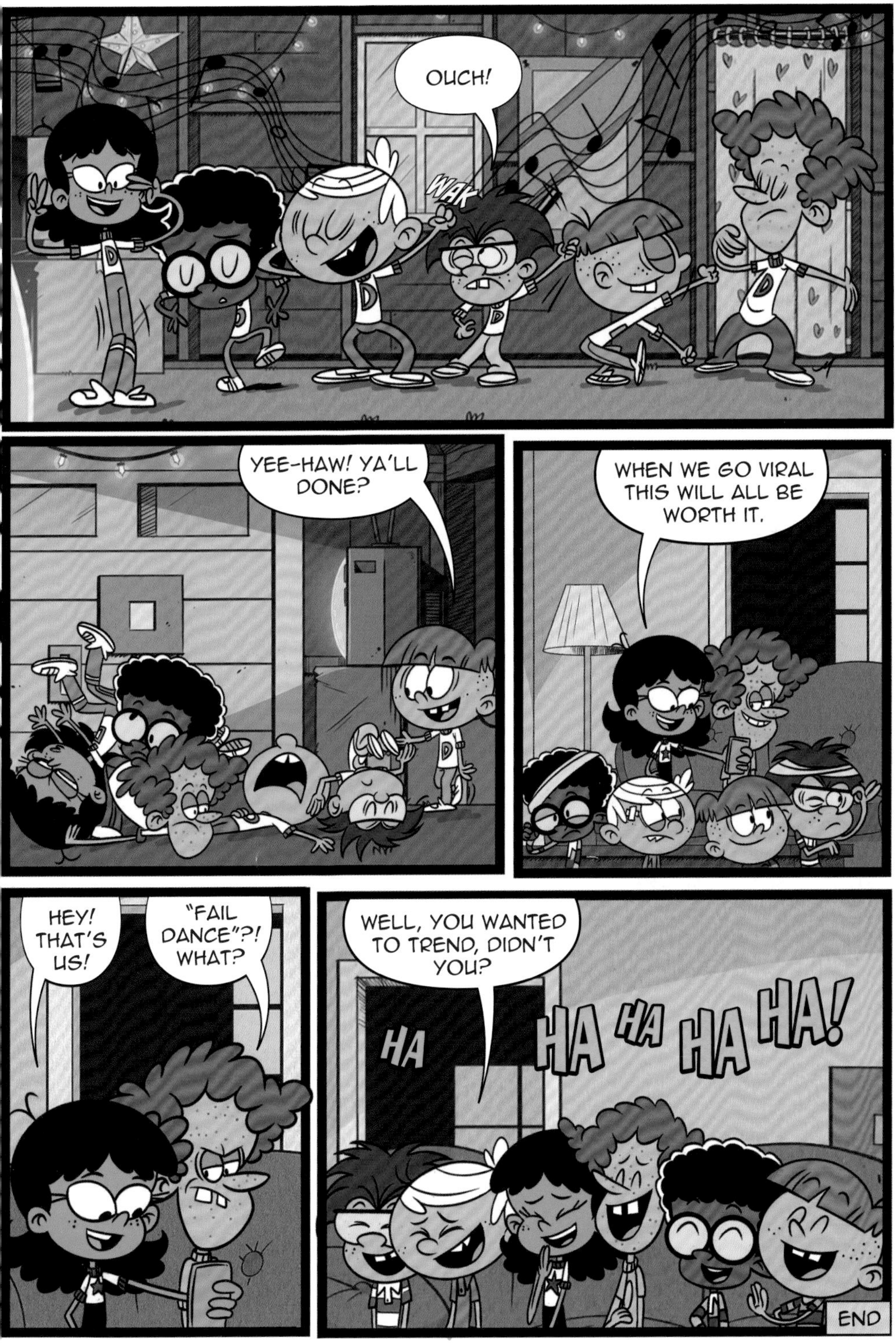
OUCH!
WAK
YEE-HAW! YA'LL DONE?
WHEN WE GO VIRAL THIS WILL ALL BE WORTH IT.
HEY! THAT'S US!
"FAIL DANCE"?! WHAT?
WELL, YOU WANTED TO TREND, DIDN'T YOU?
HA
HA HA HA HA!
END

"PROGRAM POSTPONED"

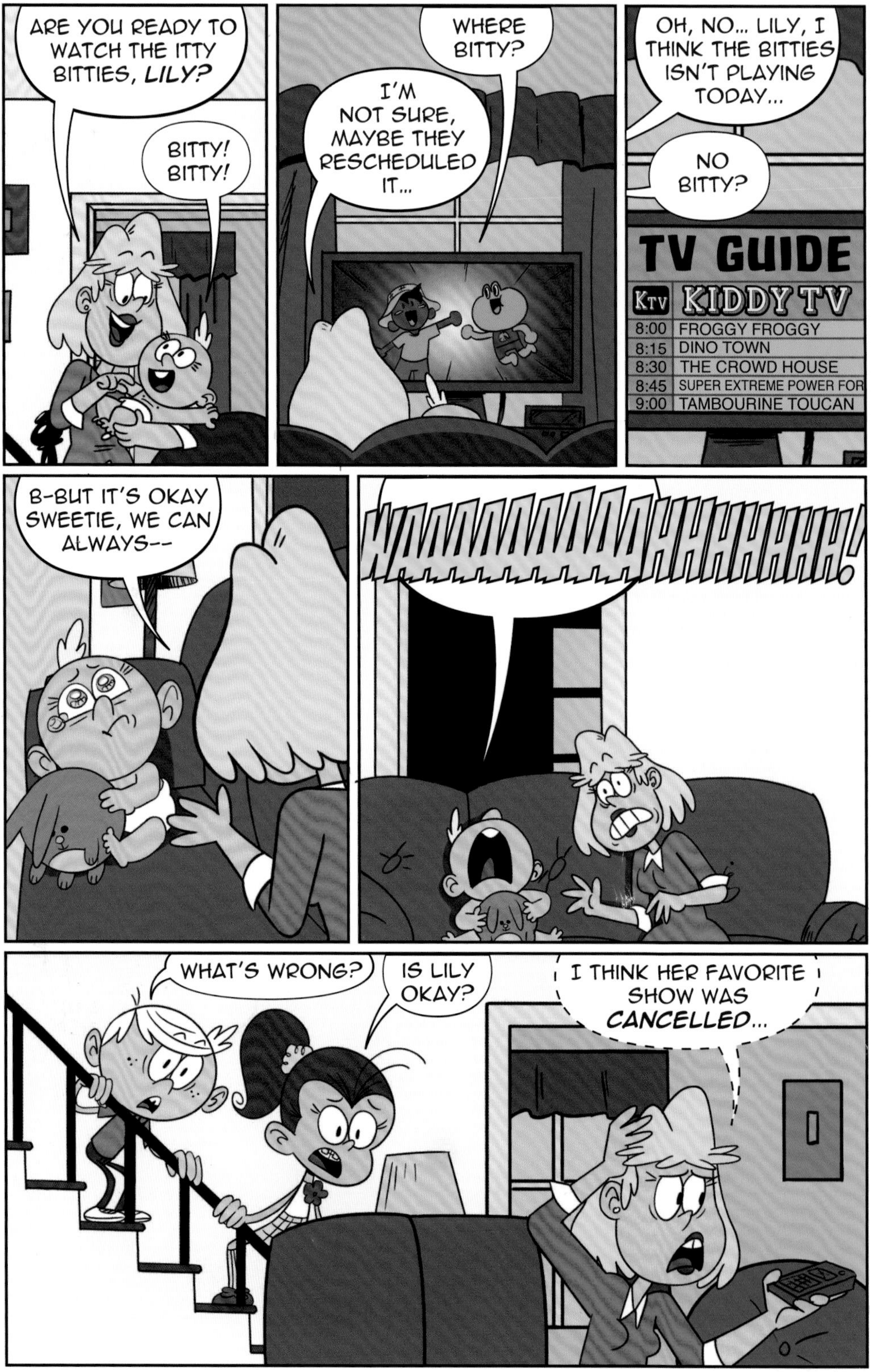
ARE YOU READY TO WATCH THE ITTY BITTIES, LILY?
BITTY! BITTY!
WHERE BITTY?
I'M NOT SURE, MAYBE THEY RESCHEDULED IT...
OH, NO... LILY, I THINK THE BITTIES ISN'T PLAYING TODAY...
NO BITTY?
TV GUIDE
KTV KIDDY TV
8:00 FROGGY FROGGY
8:15 DINO TOWN
8:30 THE CROWD HOUSE
8:45 SUPER EXTREME POWER FOR
9:00 TAMBOURINE TOUCAN
B-BUT IT'S OKAY SWEETIE, WE CAN ALWAYS--
WAAAAAAAAAAHHHHHHHH!
WHAT'S WRONG?
IS LILY OKAY?
I THINK HER FAVORITE SHOW WAS CANCELLED...

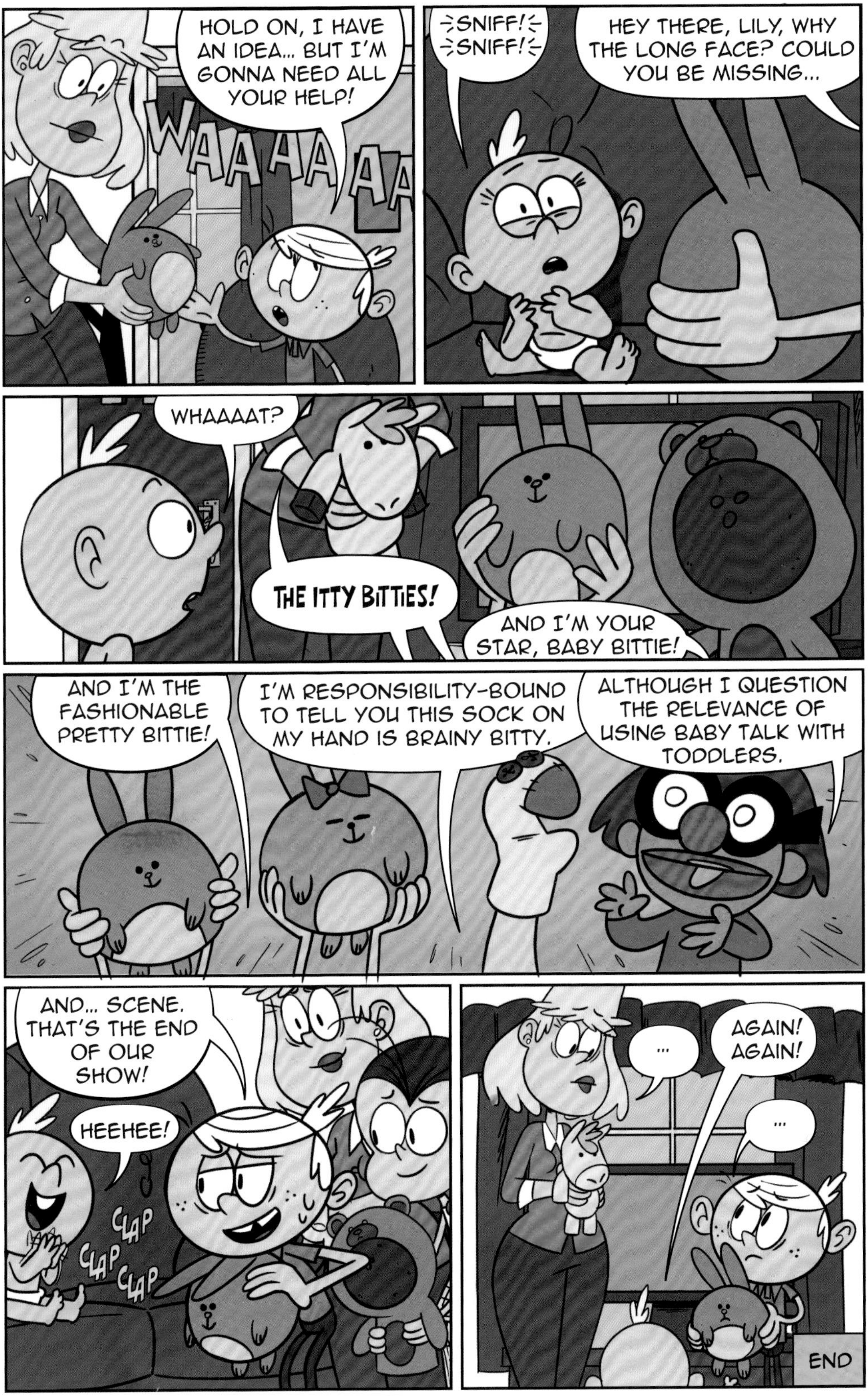
HOLD ON, I HAVE AN IDEA... BUT I'M GONNA NEED ALL YOUR HELP!
WAAAAAAA
SNIFF! SNIFF!
HEY THERE, LILY, WHY THE LONG FACE? COULD YOU BE MISSING...
WHAAAAT?
THE ITTY BITTIES!
AND I'M YOUR STAR, BABY BITTIE!
AND I'M THE FASHIONABLE PRETTY BITTIE!
I'M RESPONSIBILITY-BOUND TO TELL YOU THIS SOCK ON MY HAND IS BRAINY BITTY.
ALTHOUGH I QUESTION THE RELEVANCE OF USING BABY TALK WITH TODDLERS.
AND... SCENE. THAT'S THE END OF OUR SHOW!
HEEHEE!
CLAP CLAP CLAP
...
AGAIN! AGAIN!
...
END

"THE GOLDEN BONE"

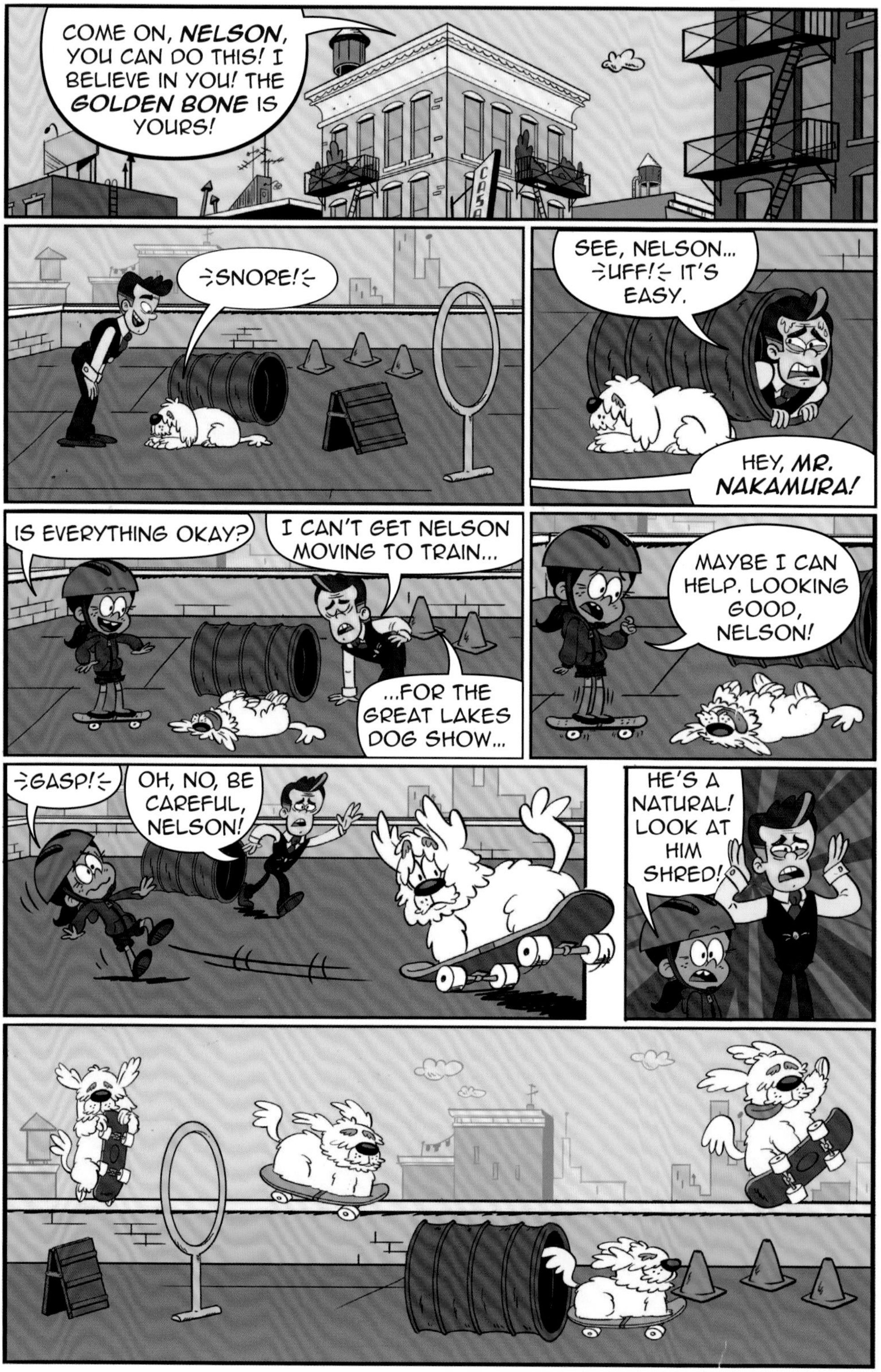

COME ON, NELSON, YOU CAN DO THIS! I BELIEVE IN YOU! THE GOLDEN BONE IS YOURS!
CASA
SNORE!
SEE, NELSON... UFF! IT'S EASY.
HEY, MR. NAKAMURA!
IS EVERYTHING OKAY?
I CAN'T GET NELSON MOVING TO TRAIN...
...FOR THE GREAT LAKES DOG SHOW...
MAYBE I CAN HELP. LOOKING GOOD, NELSON!
GASP!
OH, NO, BE CAREFUL, NELSON!
HE'S A NATURAL! LOOK AT HIM SHRED!

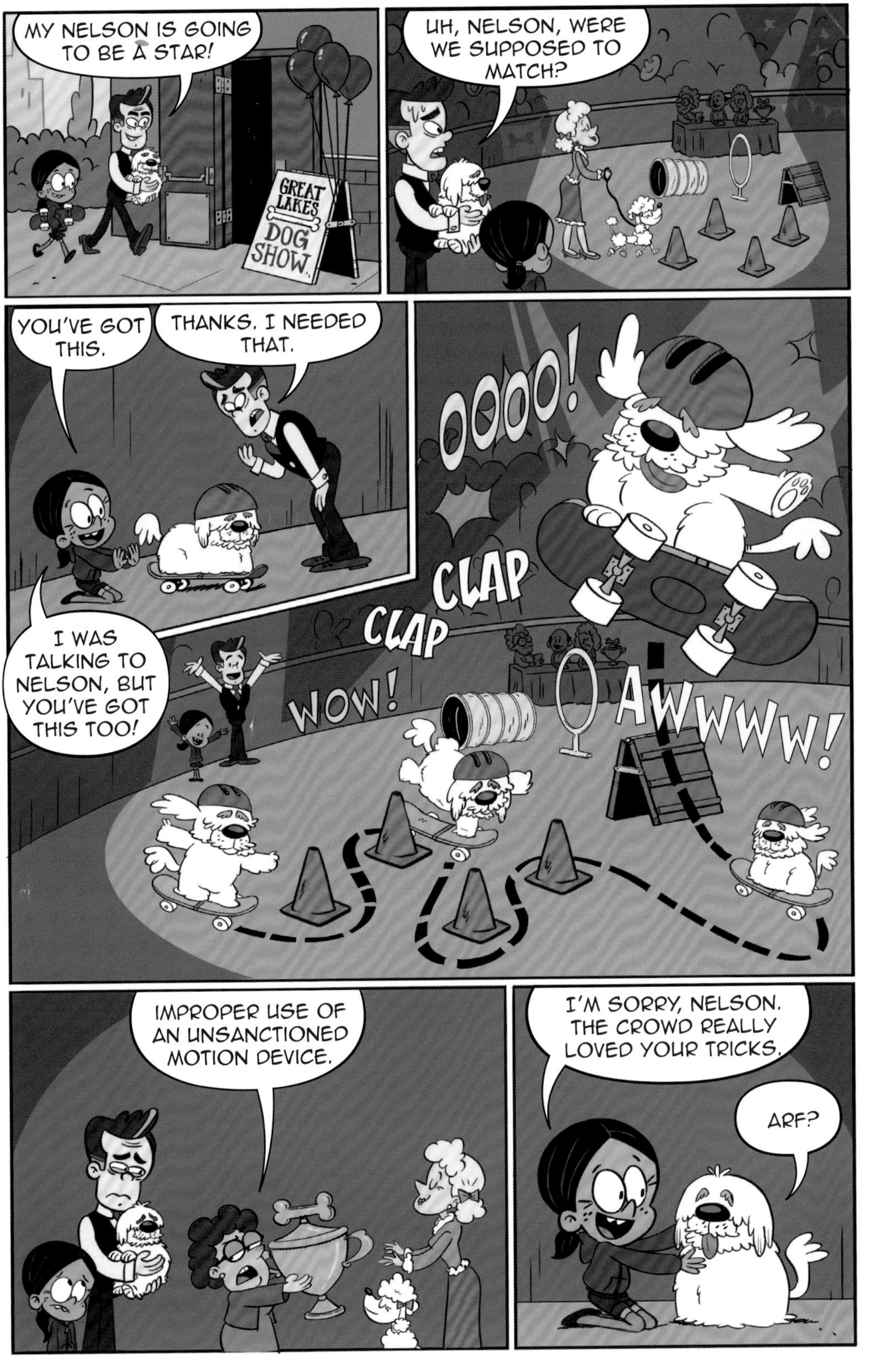
MY NELSON IS GOING TO BE A STAR!
GREAT LAKES DOG SHOW
UH, NELSON, WERE WE SUPPOSED TO MATCH?
YOU'VE GOT THIS.
THANKS. I NEEDED THAT.
I WAS TALKING TO NELSON, BUT YOU'VE GOT THIS TOO!
OOOO!
CLAP
CLAP
WOW!
AWWWWW!
IMPROPER USE OF AN UNSANCTIONED MOTION DEVICE.
I'M SORRY, NELSON. THE CROWD REALLY LOVED YOUR TRICKS.
ARF?

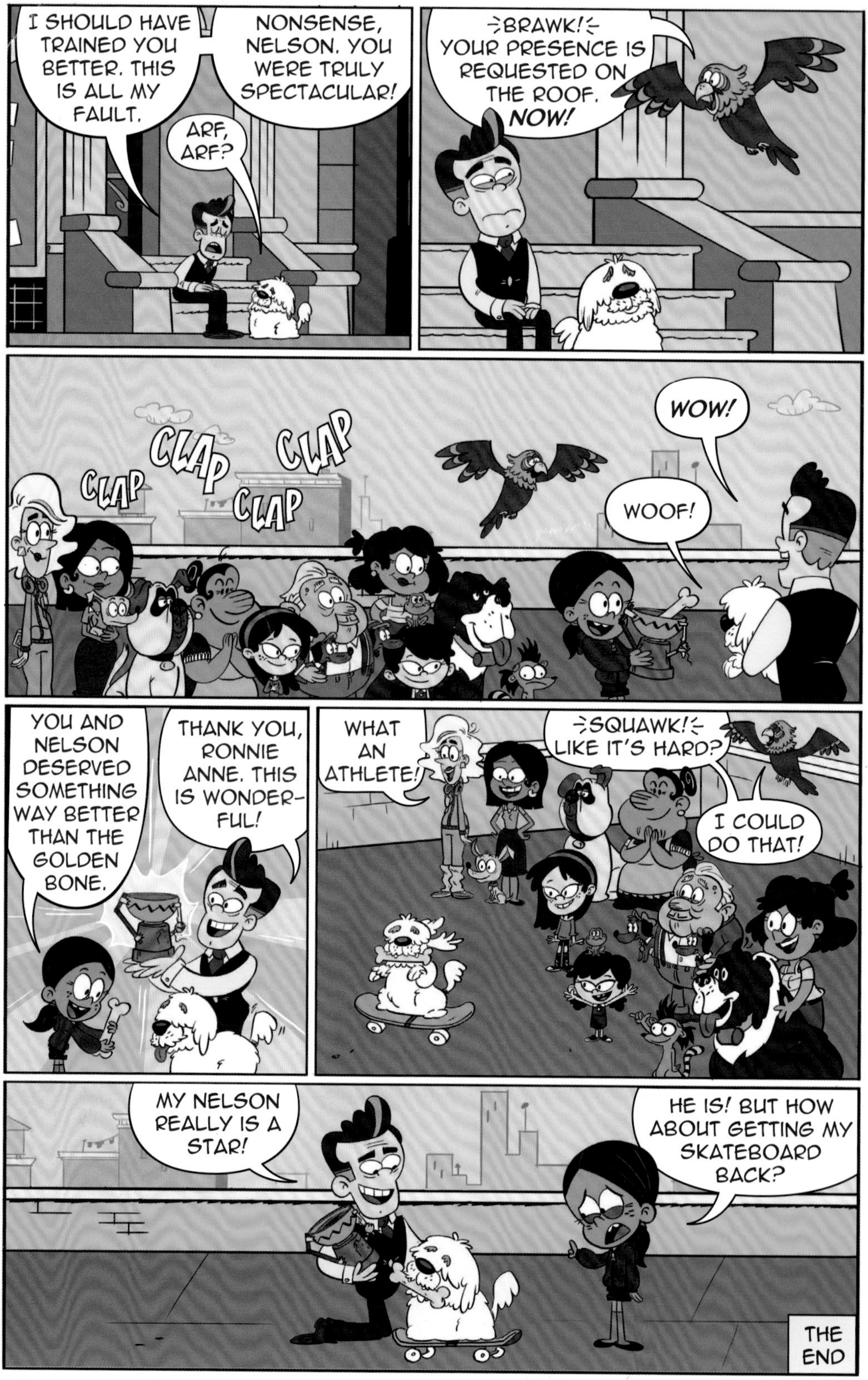
I SHOULD HAVE TRAINED YOU BETTER. THIS IS ALL MY FAULT.
NONSENSE, NELSON. YOU WERE TRULY SPECTACULAR!
ARF, ARF?
BRAWK! YOUR PRESENCE IS REQUESTED ON THE ROOF. NOW!
CLAP
CLAP
CLAP
CLAP
WOW!
WOOF!
YOU AND NELSON DESERVED SOMETHING WAY BETTER THAN THE GOLDEN BONE.
THANK YOU, RONNIE ANNE. THIS IS WONDER-FUL!
WHAT AN ATHLETE!
SQUAWK! LIKE IT'S HARD?
I COULD DO THAT!
MY NELSON REALLY IS A STAR!
HE IS! BUT HOW ABOUT GETTING MY SKATEBOARD BACK?
THE END

"SO SUBLIMINAL"

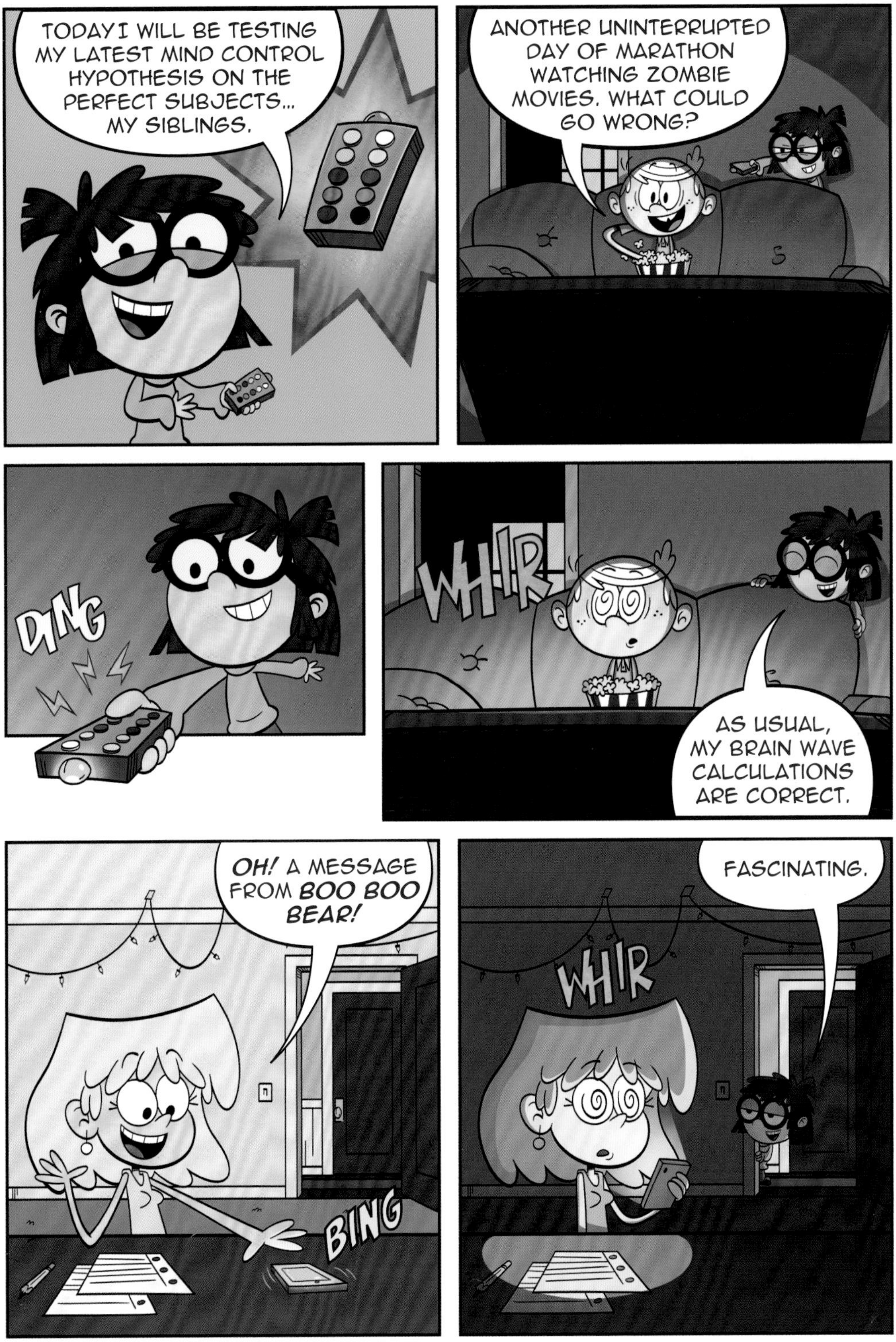

TODAY I WILL BE TESTING MY LATEST MIND CONTROL HYPOTHESIS ON THE PERFECT SUBJECTS... MY SIBLINGS.
ANOTHER UNINTERRUPTED DAY OF MARATHON WATCHING ZOMBIE MOVIES. WHAT COULD GO WRONG?
DING
WHIR
AS USUAL, MY BRAIN WAVE CALCULATIONS ARE CORRECT.
OH! A MESSAGE FROM BOO BOO BEAR!
BING
WHIR
FASCINATING.

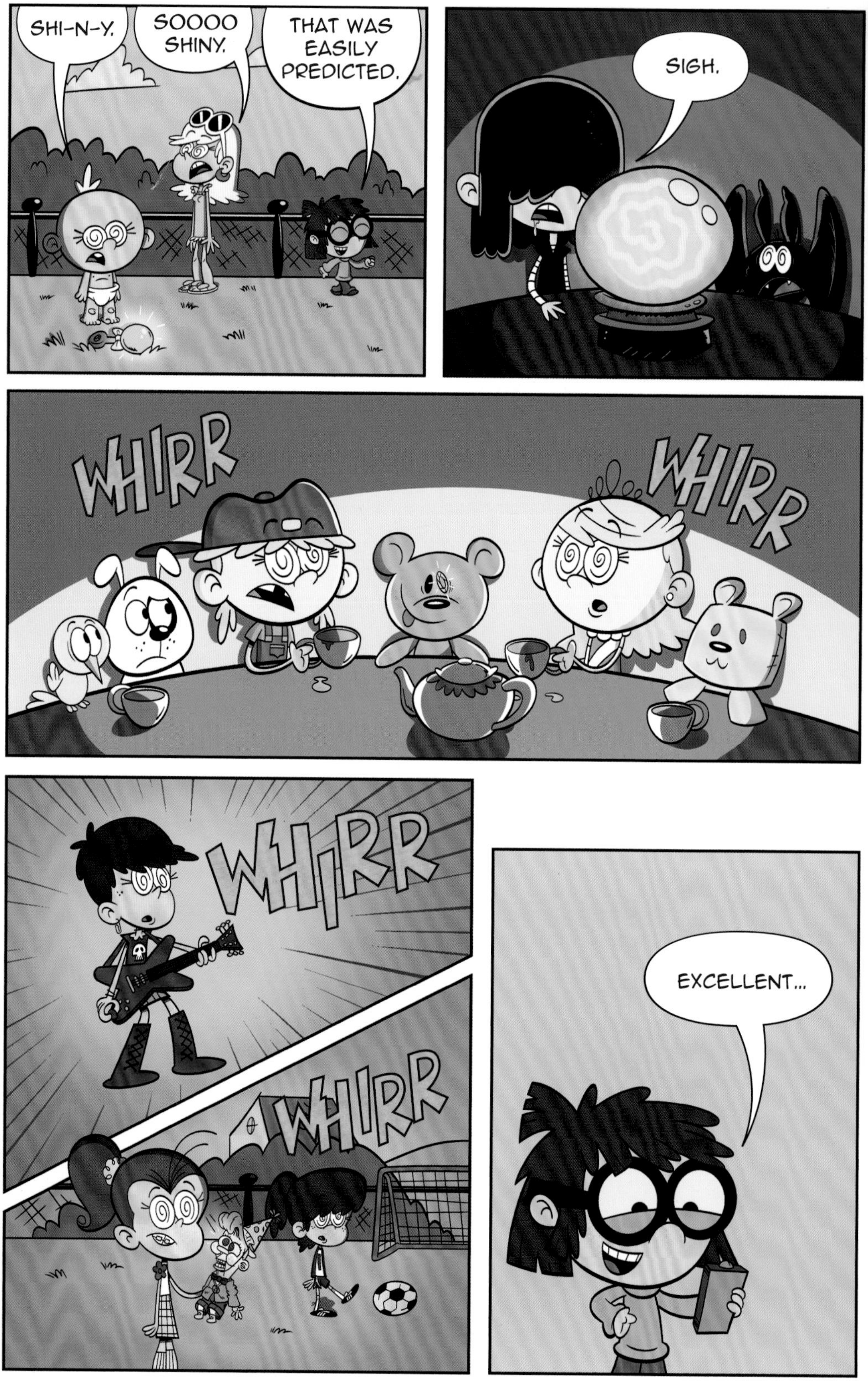
SHI-N-Y.
SOOOO SHINY.
THAT WAS EASILY PREDICTED.
SIGH.
WHIRR
WHIRR
WHIRR
WHIRR
EXCELLENT...

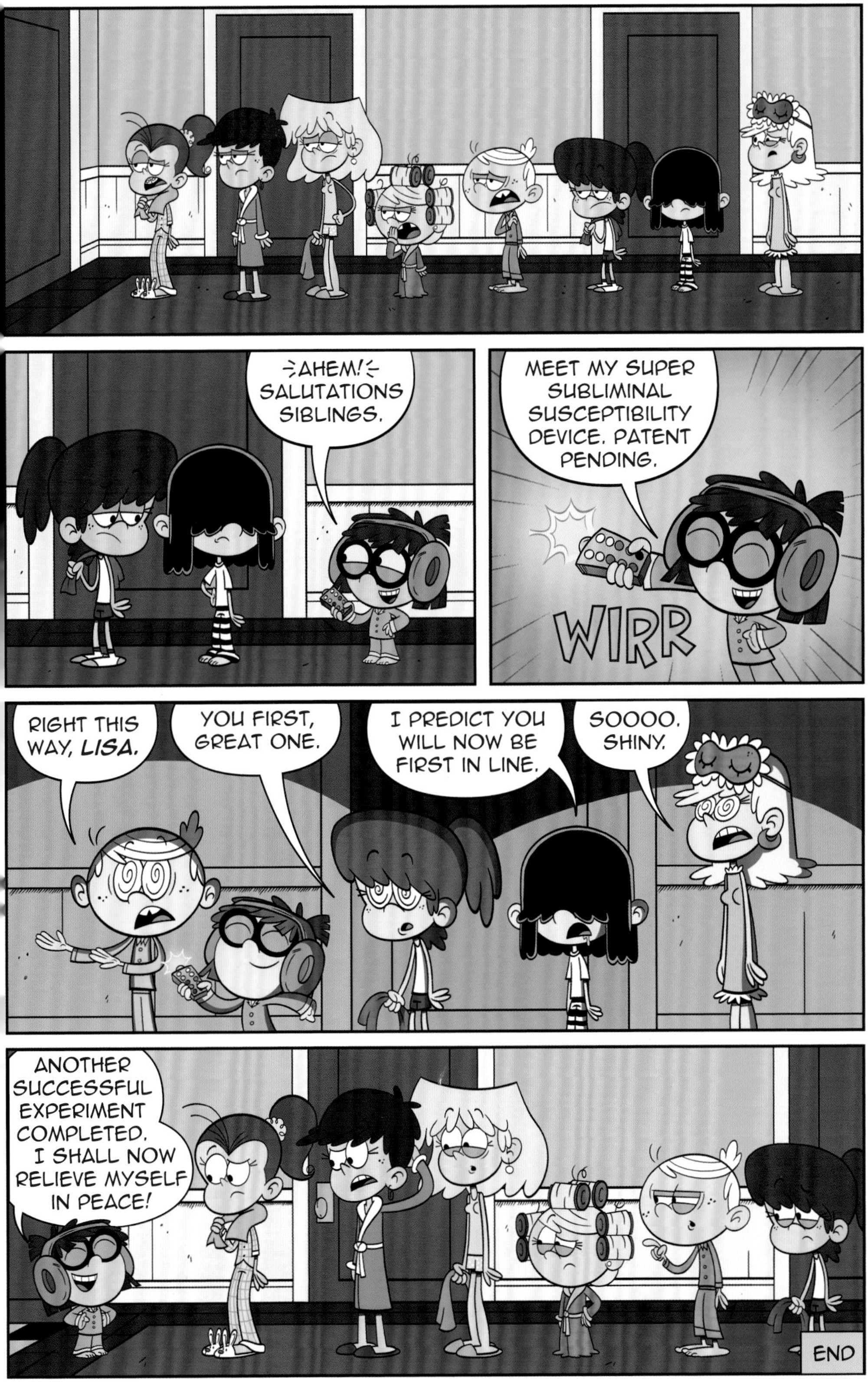
AHEM!
SALUTATIONS SIBLINGS.
MEET MY SUPER SUBLIMINAL SUSCEPTIBILITY DEVICE. PATENT PENDING.
WIRR
RIGHT THIS WAY, LISA.
YOU FIRST, GREAT ONE.
I PREDICT YOU WILL NOW BE FIRST IN LINE.
SOOOO. SHINY.
ANOTHER SUCCESSFUL EXPERIMENT COMPLETED. I SHALL NOW RELIEVE MYSELF IN PEACE!
END

"TICKET FOR TWO"

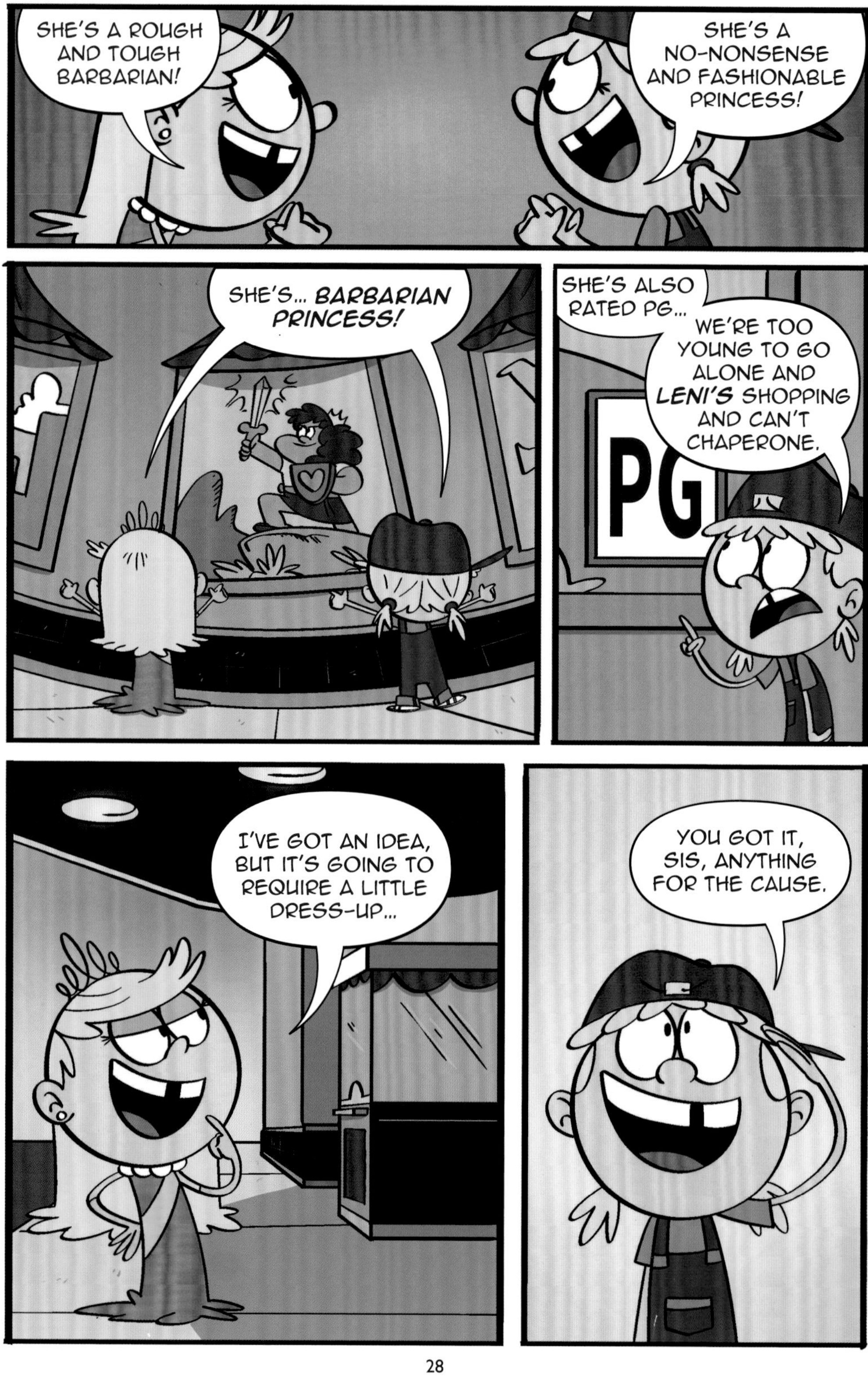
SHE'S A ROUGH AND TOUGH BARBARIAN!
SHE'S A NO-NONSENSE AND FASHIONABLE PRINCESS!
SHE'S... BARBARIAN PRINCESS!
SHE'S ALSO RATED PG...
WE'RE TOO YOUNG TO GO ALONE AND LENI'S SHOPPING AND CAN'T CHAPERONE.
PG
I'VE GOT AN IDEA, BUT IT'S GOING TO REQUIRE A LITTLE DRESS-UP...
YOU GOT IT, SIS, ANYTHING FOR THE CAUSE.

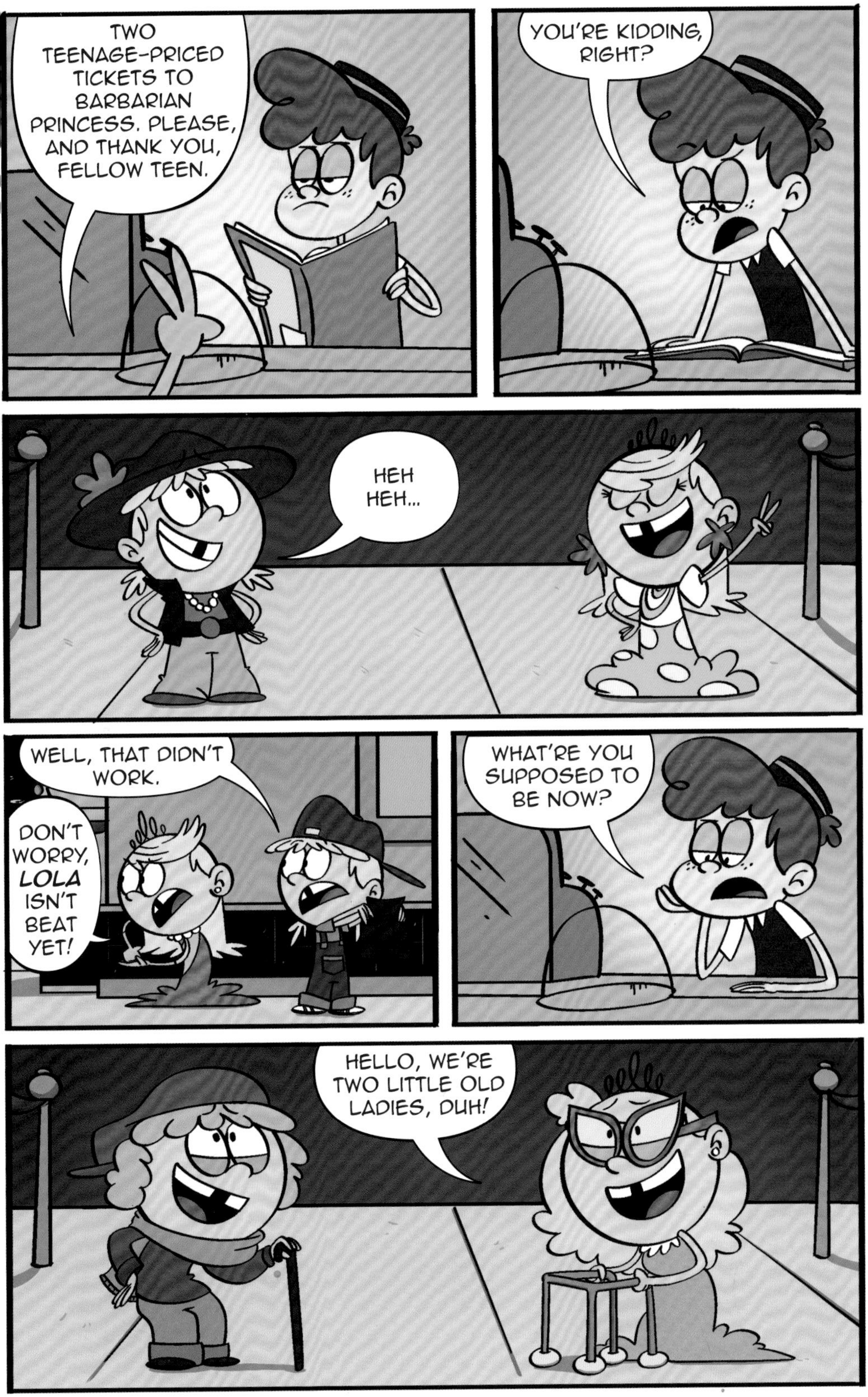

TWO TEENAGE-PRICED TICKETS TO BARBARIAN PRINCESS. PLEASE, AND THANK YOU, FELLOW TEEN.
YOU'RE KIDDING, RIGHT?
HEH HEH...
WELL, THAT DIDN'T WORK.
DON'T WORRY, LOLA ISN'T BEAT YET!
WHAT'RE YOU SUPPOSED TO BE NOW?
HELLO, WE'RE TWO LITTLE OLD LADIES, DUH!

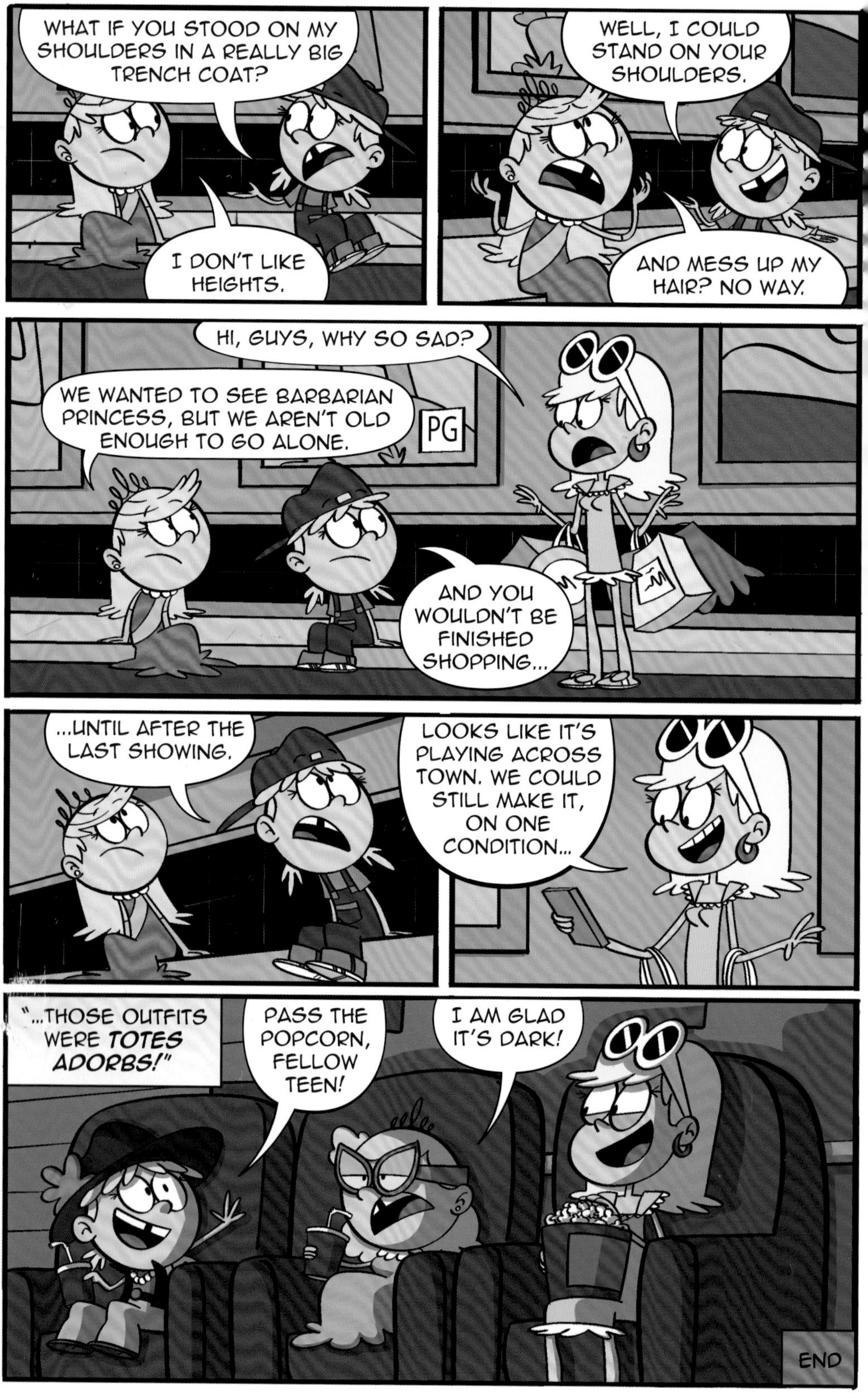
WHAT IF YOU STOOD ON MY SHOULDERS IN A REALLY BIG TRENCH COAT?
I DON'T LIKE HEIGHTS.
WELL, I COULD STAND ON YOUR SHOULDERS.
AND MESS UP MY HAIR? NO WAY.
HI, GUYS, WHY SO SAD?
WE WANTED TO SEE BARBARIAN PRINCESS, BUT WE AREN'T OLD ENOUGH TO GO ALONE.
PG
AND YOU WOULDN'T BE FINISHED SHOPPING...
...UNTIL AFTER THE LAST SHOWING.
LOOKS LIKE IT'S PLAYING ACROSS TOWN. WE COULD STILL MAKE IT, ON ONE CONDITION...
"...THOSE OUTFITS WERE *TOTES ADORBS!*"
PASS THE POPCORN, FELLOW TEEN!
I AM GLAD IT'S DARK!
END

"BOBBY'S WORLD"

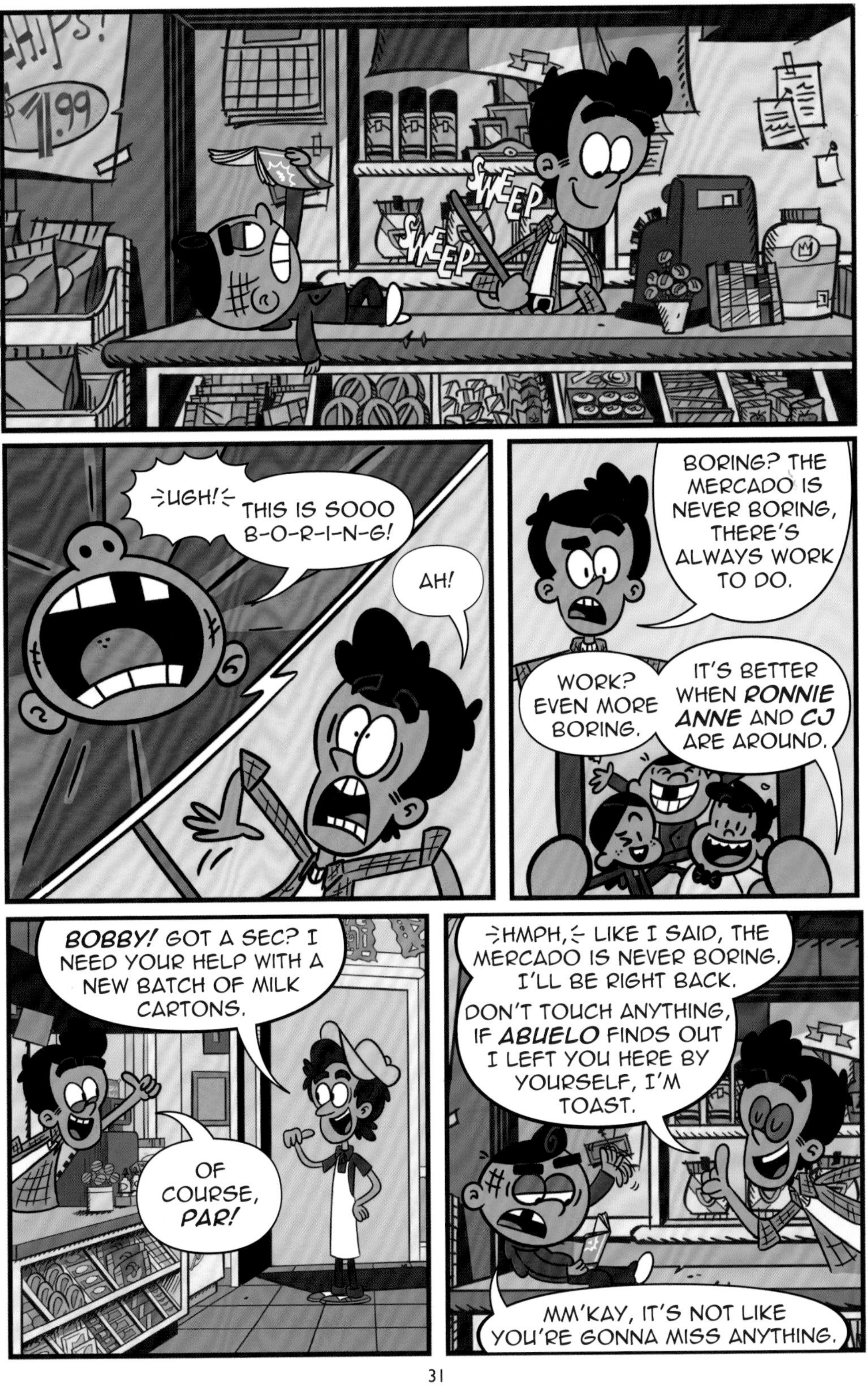

CHIPS!
$1.99
SWEEP
SWEEP
UGH!
THIS IS SOOO B-O-R-I-N-G!
AH!
BORING? THE MERCADO IS NEVER BORING, THERE'S ALWAYS WORK TO DO.
WORK? EVEN MORE BORING.
IT'S BETTER WHEN *RONNIE ANNE* AND *CJ* ARE AROUND.
BOBBY! GOT A SEC? I NEED YOUR HELP WITH A NEW BATCH OF MILK CARTONS.
OF COURSE, *PAR!*
HMPH, LIKE I SAID, THE MERCADO IS NEVER BORING. I'LL BE RIGHT BACK.
DON'T TOUCH ANYTHING, IF *ABUELO* FINDS OUT I LEFT YOU HERE BY YOURSELF, I'M TOAST.
MM'KAY, IT'S NOT LIKE YOU'RE GONNA MISS ANYTHING.

:SIGH!:

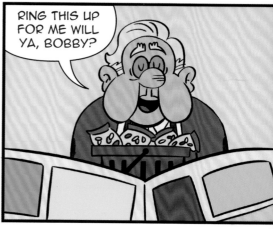

RING THIS UP FOR ME WILL YA, BOBBY?

"BOBBY"?!

THANKS FOR ALWAYS HAVING THESE JELLY BEANS, THEY'RE HARD TO FIND!

ZIP

LOST

BY THE WAY... YOU JUST RAN OUT. MIGHT WANNA GET SOME MORE.

UH...YEAH, SURE.

HEH. ALL SET, *VITO!*

LOOKS LIKE YOU GOT A CALL THERE. SO LONG, BOBBY!

Special Ice cream 9¢

BZZZT

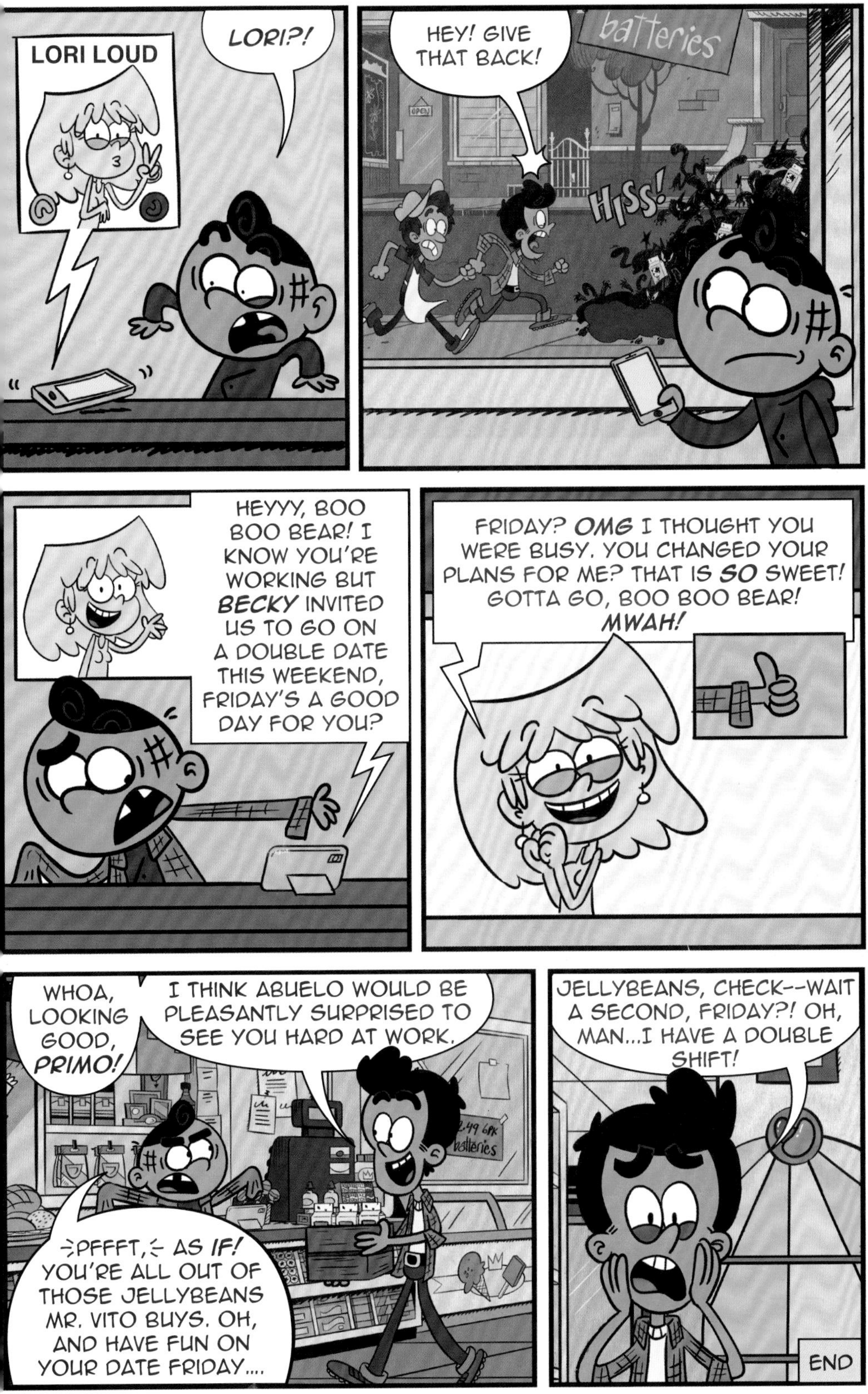
LORI LOUD
LORI?!
HEY! GIVE THAT BACK!
batteries
HISS!
HEYYY, BOO BOO BEAR! I KNOW YOU'RE WORKING BUT BECKY INVITED US TO GO ON A DOUBLE DATE THIS WEEKEND, FRIDAY'S A GOOD DAY FOR YOU?
FRIDAY? OMG I THOUGHT YOU WERE BUSY. YOU CHANGED YOUR PLANS FOR ME? THAT IS SO SWEET! GOTTA GO, BOO BOO BEAR! MWAH!
WHOA, LOOKING GOOD, PRIMO!
I THINK ABUELO WOULD BE PLEASANTLY SURPRISED TO SEE YOU HARD AT WORK.
PFFFT, AS IF! YOU'RE ALL OUT OF THOSE JELLYBEANS MR. VITO BUYS. OH, AND HAVE FUN ON YOUR DATE FRIDAY....
JELLYBEANS, CHECK--WAIT A SECOND, FRIDAY?! OH, MAN...I HAVE A DOUBLE SHIFT!
END

"ON THE HUSH HUSH"

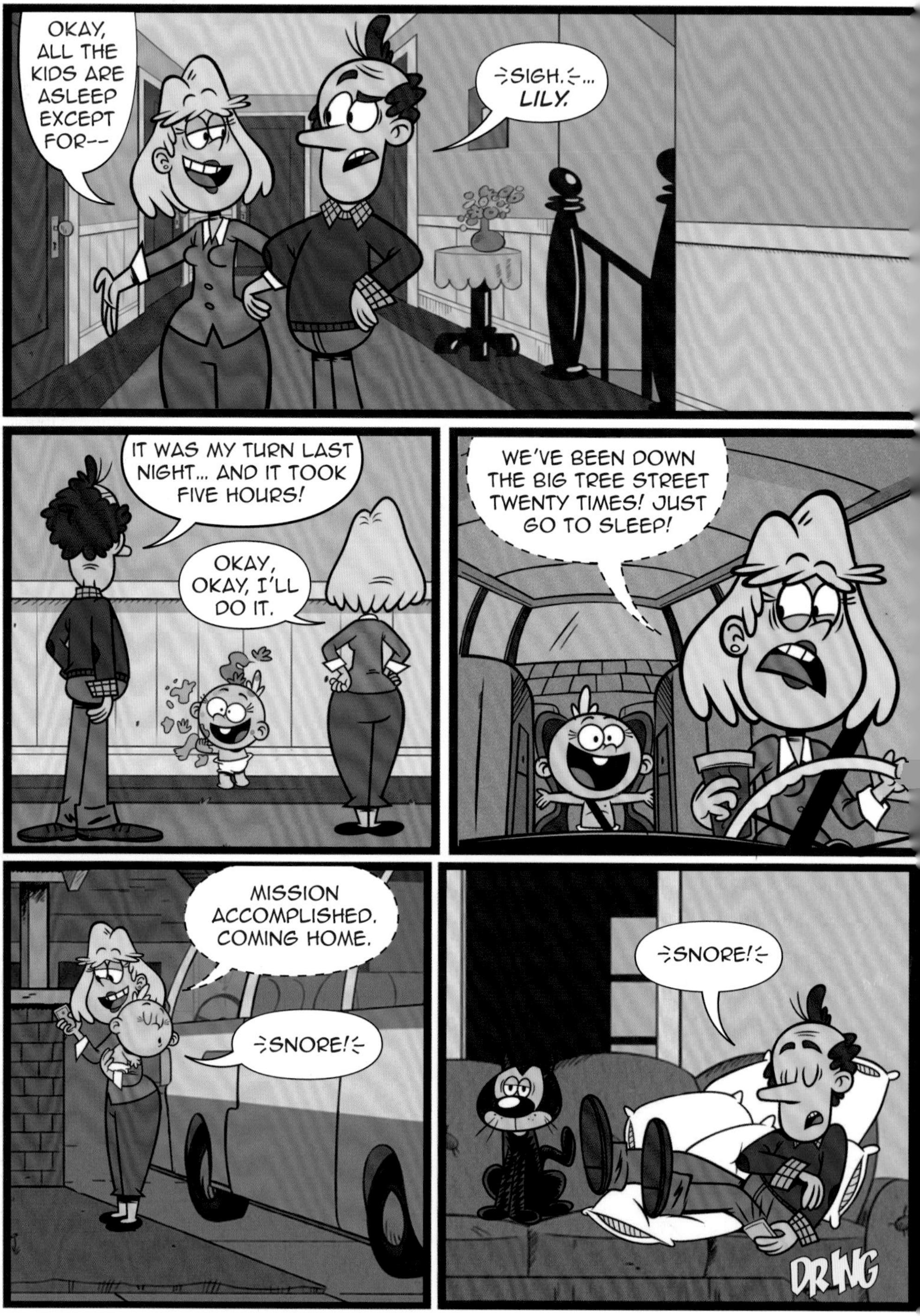
OKAY, ALL THE KIDS ARE ASLEEP EXCEPT FOR--
SIGH. ... LILY.
IT WAS MY TURN LAST NIGHT... AND IT TOOK FIVE HOURS!
OKAY, OKAY, I'LL DO IT.
WE'VE BEEN DOWN THE BIG TREE STREET TWENTY TIMES! JUST GO TO SLEEP!
MISSION ACCOMPLISHED. COMING HOME.
SNORE!
SNORE!
DRING

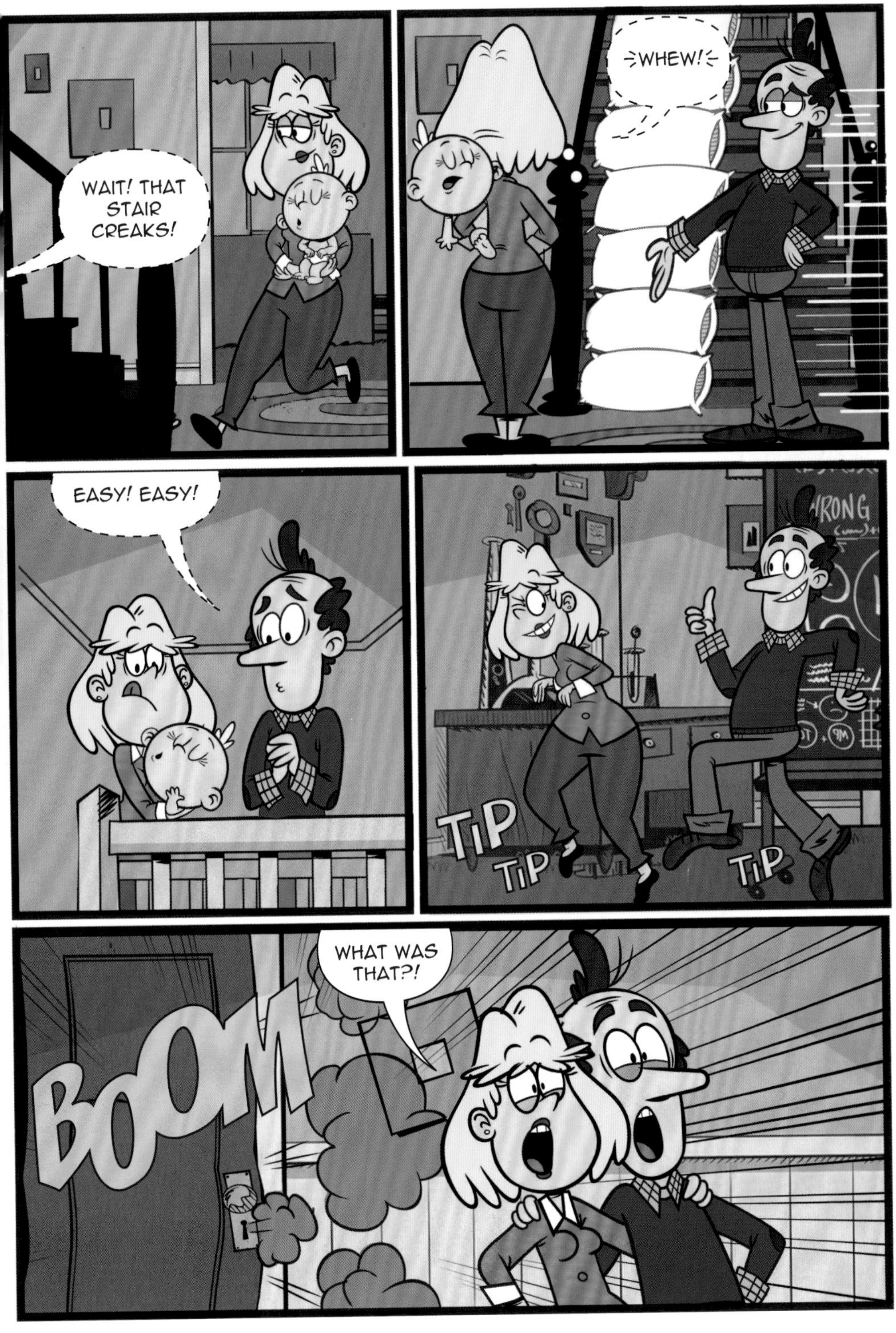
WAIT! THAT STAIR CREAKS!
WHEW!
EASY! EASY!
TIP
TIP
TIP
BOOM
WHAT WAS THAT?!

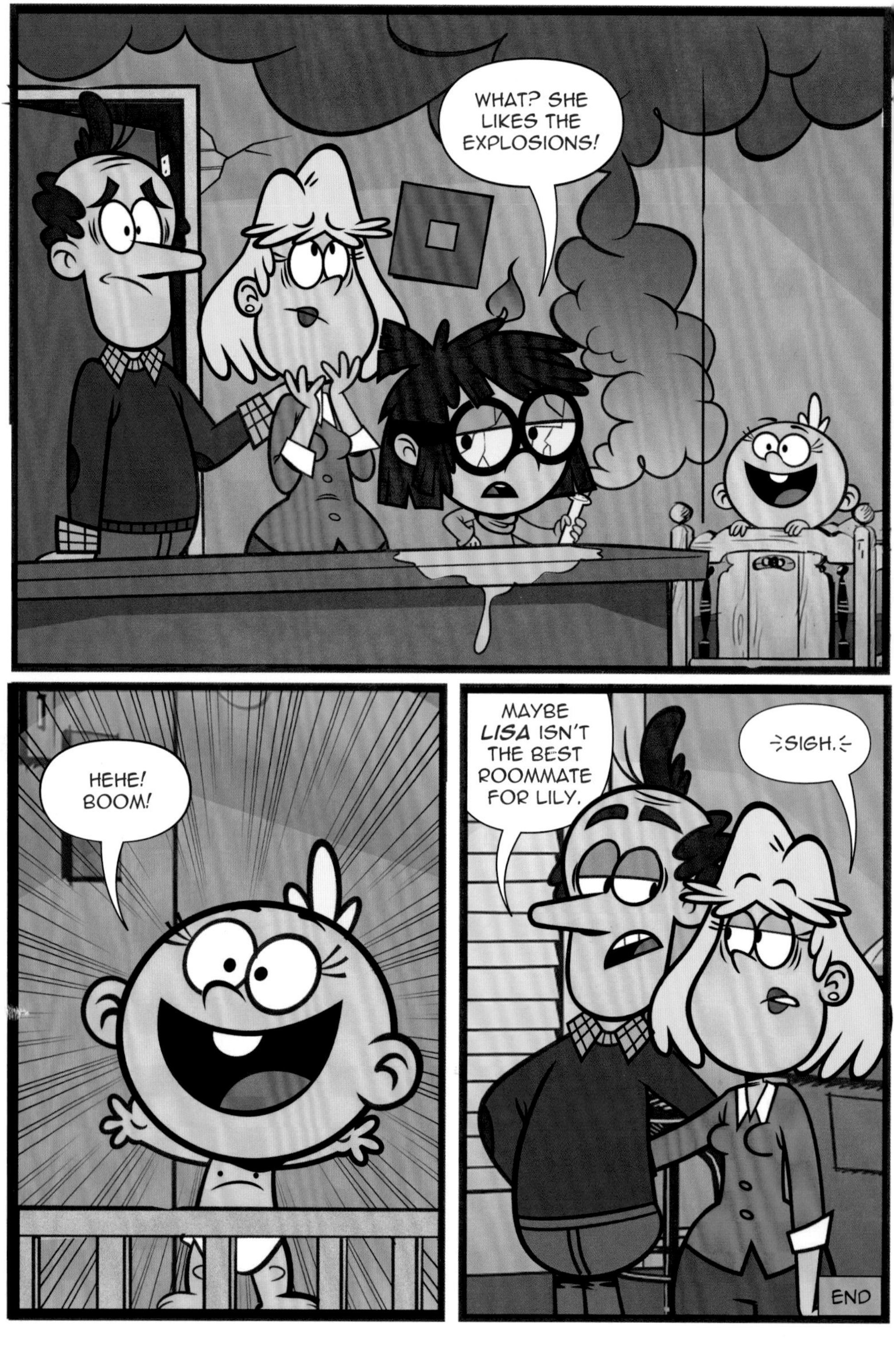
WHAT? SHE LIKES THE EXPLOSIONS!
HEHE! BOOM!
MAYBE LISA ISN'T THE BEST ROOMMATE FOR LILY.
SIGH.
END

COUNTRY MOUSE, SUBURBAN HAMSTER"

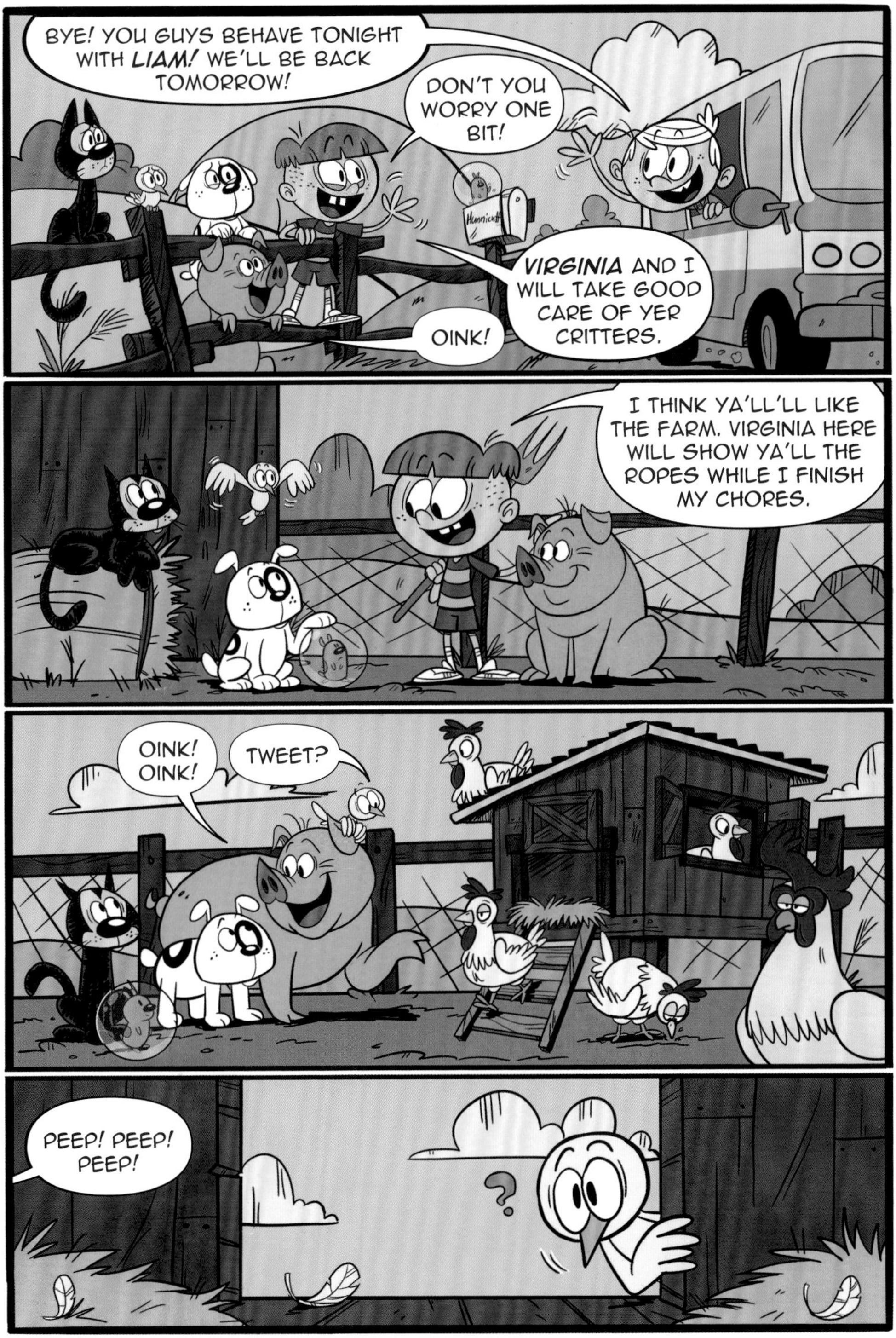
BYE! YOU GUYS BEHAVE TONIGHT WITH *LIAM!* WE'LL BE BACK TOMORROW!
DON'T YOU WORRY ONE BIT!
VIRGINIA AND I WILL TAKE GOOD CARE OF YER CRITTERS.
OINK!
I THINK YA'LL'LL LIKE THE FARM. VIRGINIA HERE WILL SHOW YA'LL THE ROPES WHILE I FINISH MY CHORES.
OINK! OINK!
TWEET?
PEEP! PEEP! PEEP!

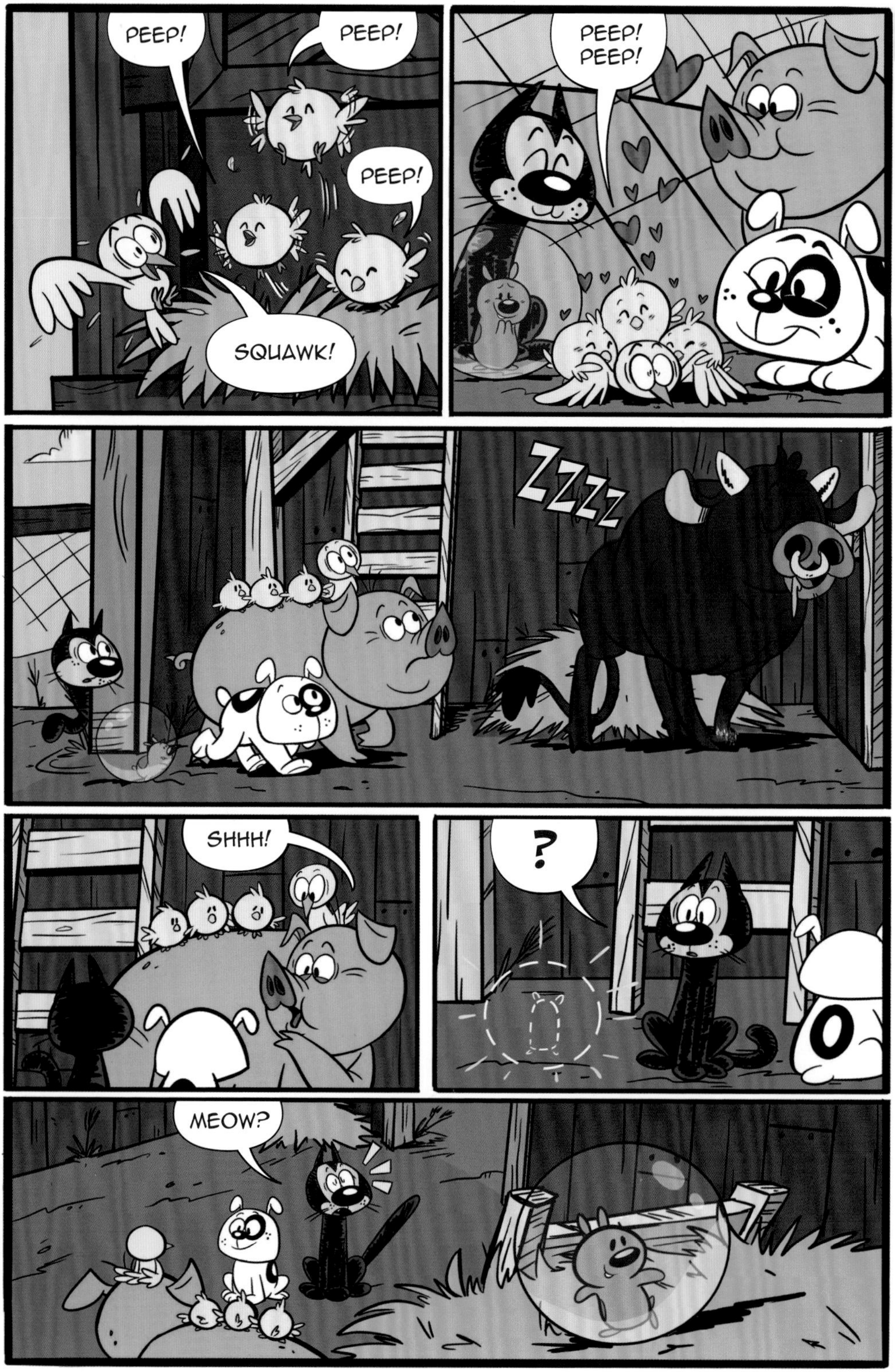
PEEP!
PEEP!
PEEP!
SQUAWK!
PEEP!
PEEP!
ZZZZ
SHHH!
?
MEOW?

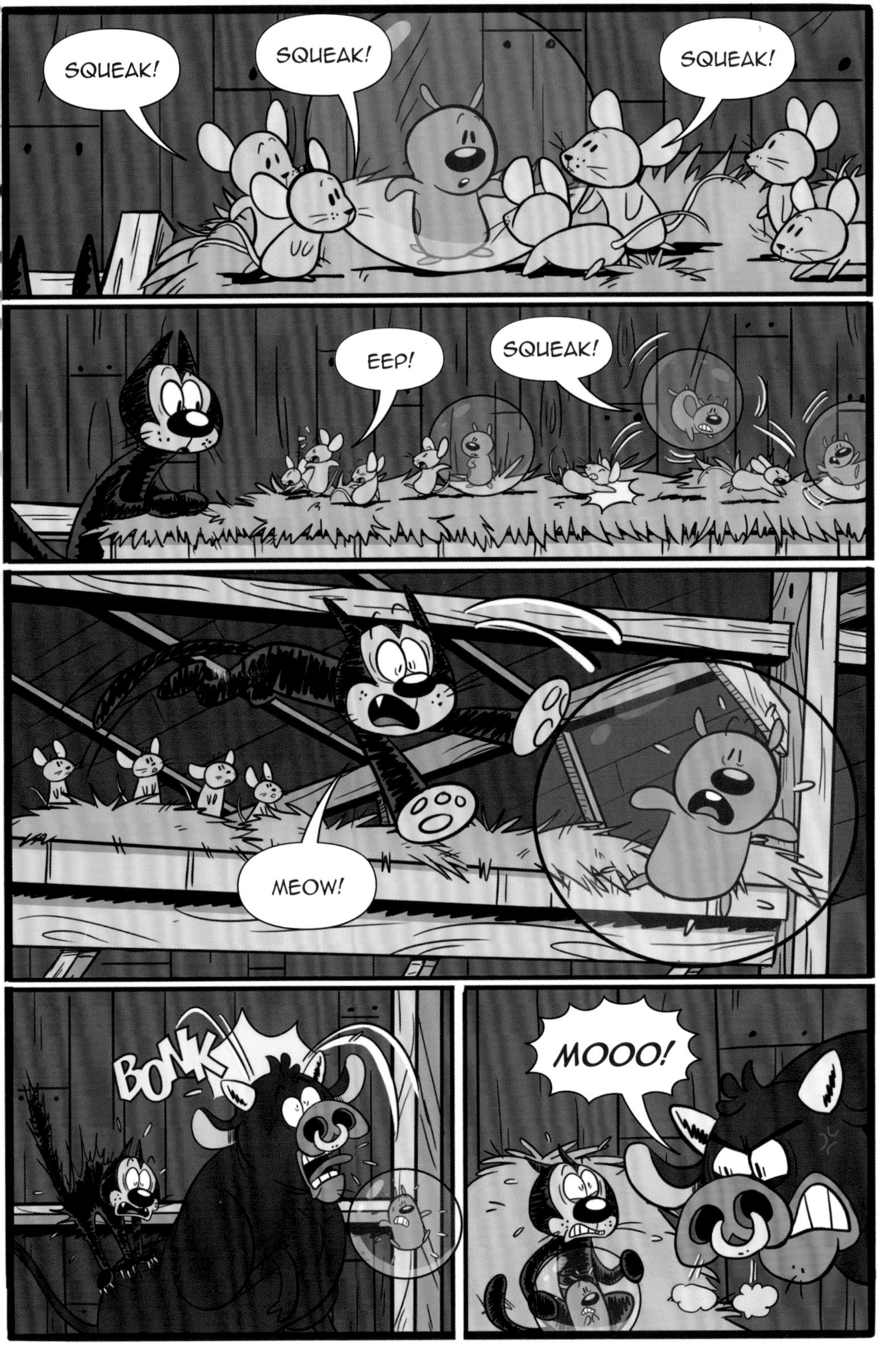
SQUEAK!
SQUEAK!
SQUEAK!
EEP!
SQUEAK!
MEOW!
BONK
MOOO!

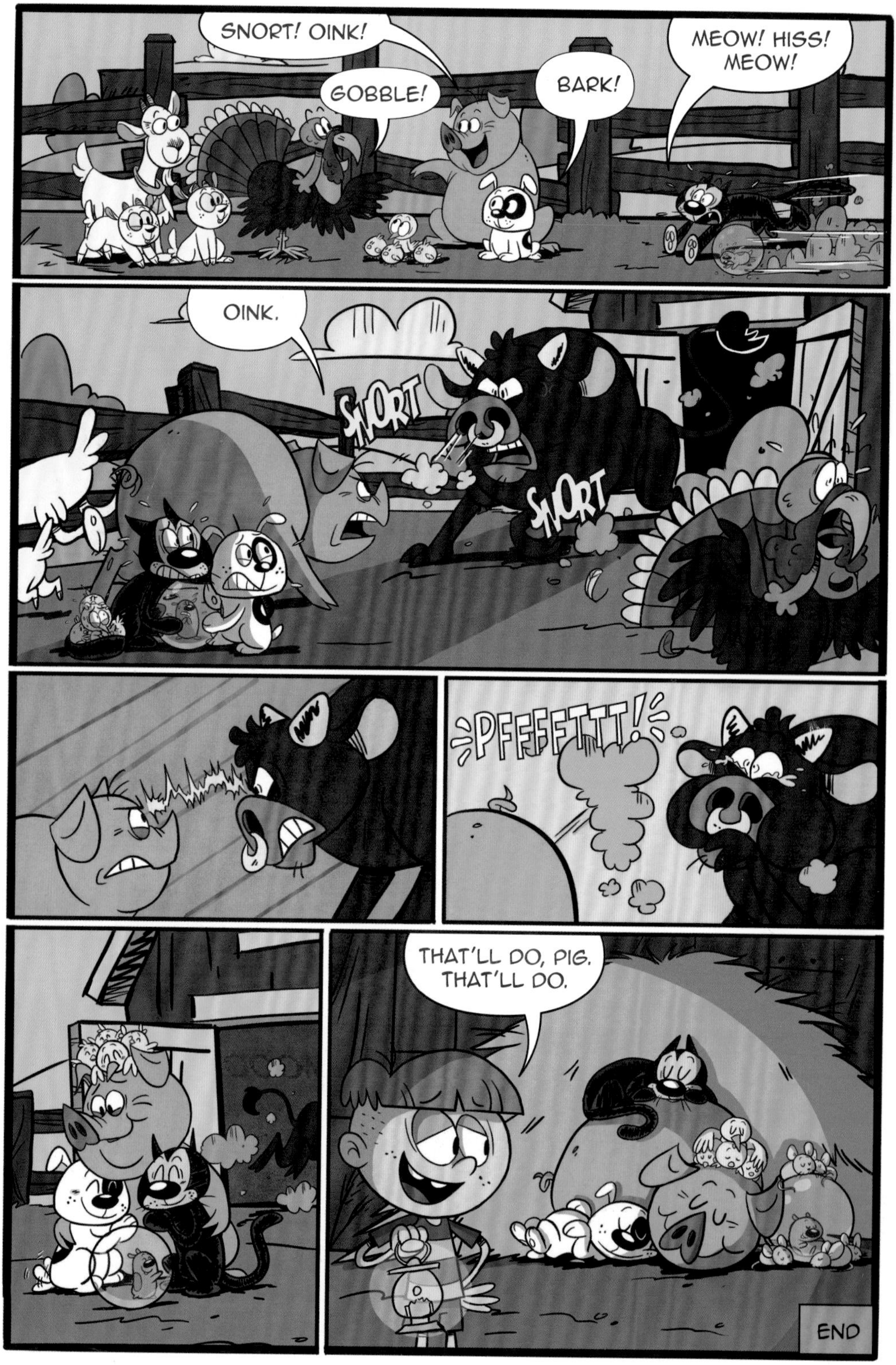
SNORT! OINK!
GOBBLE!
BARK!
MEOW! HISS! MEOW!
OINK.
SNORT
SNORT
PFFFFTTT!
THAT'LL DO, PIG. THAT'LL DO.
END

"WALKMAN THE LINE"

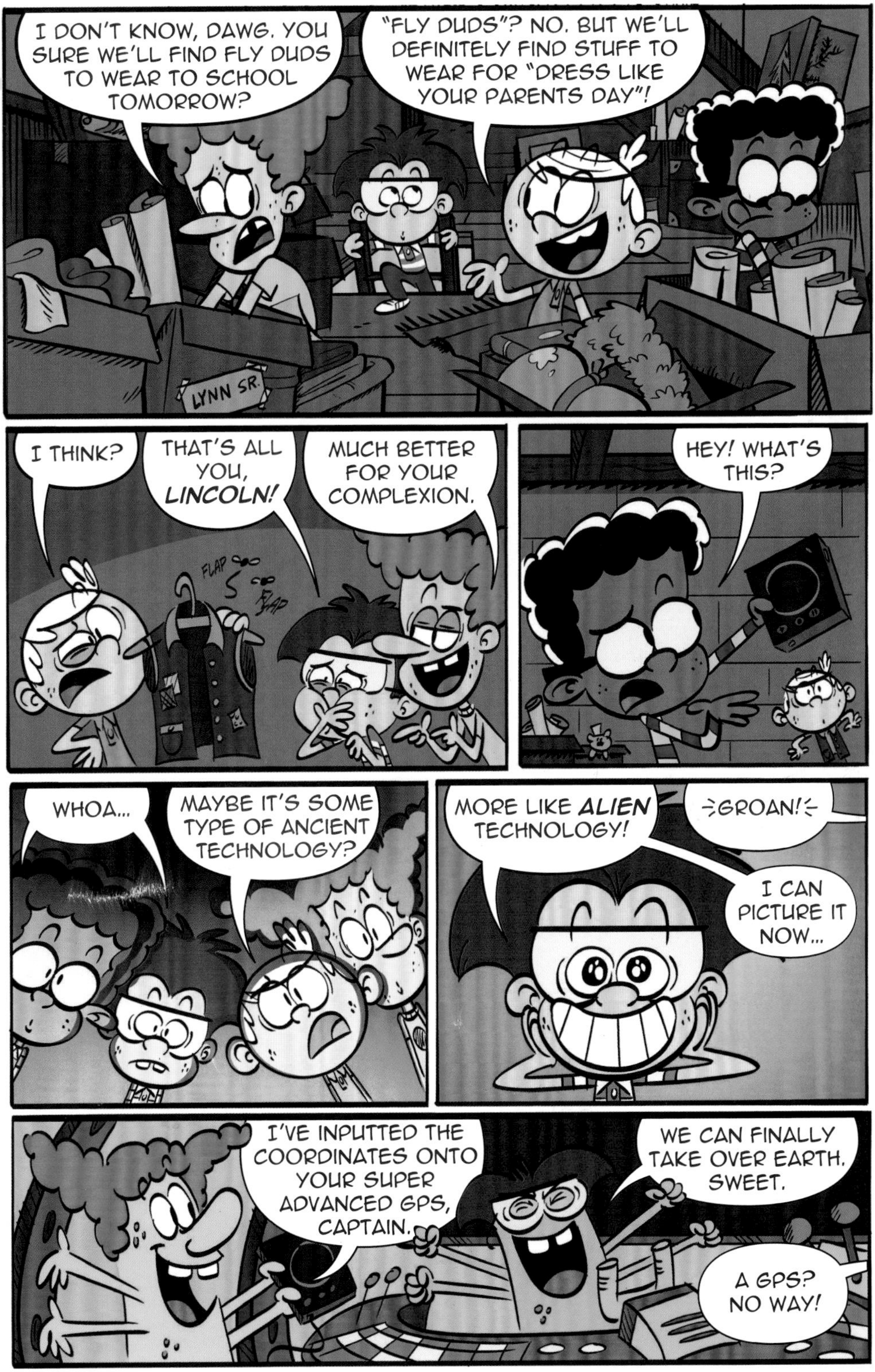
I DON'T KNOW, DAWG. YOU SURE WE'LL FIND FLY DUDS TO WEAR TO SCHOOL TOMORROW?
"FLY DUDS"? NO. BUT WE'LL DEFINITELY FIND STUFF TO WEAR FOR "DRESS LIKE YOUR PARENTS DAY"!
LYNN SR.
I THINK?
THAT'S ALL YOU, LINCOLN!
MUCH BETTER FOR YOUR COMPLEXION.
FLAP
FLAP
HEY! WHAT'S THIS?
WHOA...
MAYBE IT'S SOME TYPE OF ANCIENT TECHNOLOGY?
MORE LIKE ALIEN TECHNOLOGY!
GROAN!
I CAN PICTURE IT NOW...
I'VE INPUTTED THE COORDINATES ONTO YOUR SUPER ADVANCED GPS, CAPTAIN.
WE CAN FINALLY TAKE OVER EARTH. SWEET.
A GPS? NO WAY!

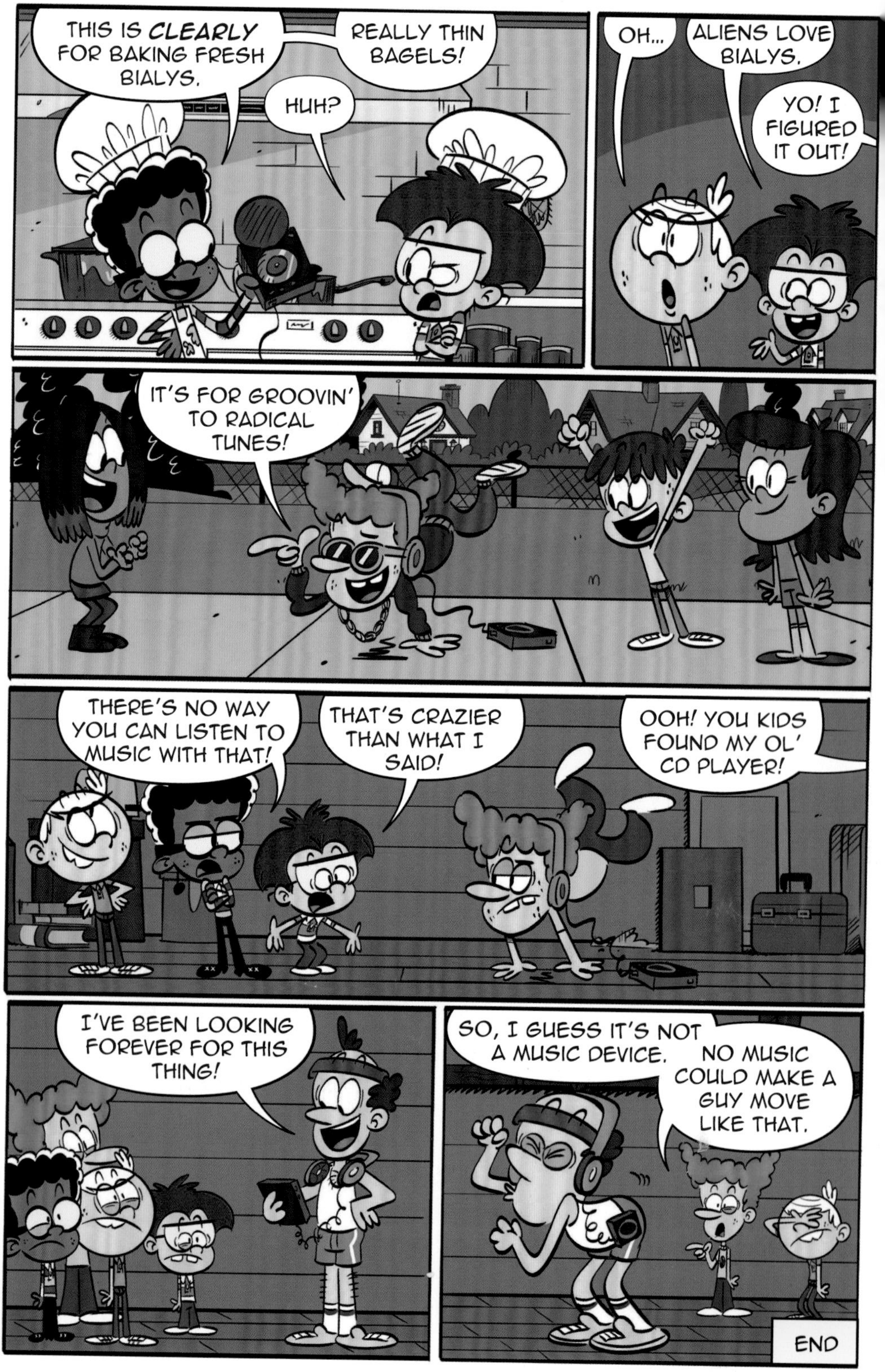
THIS IS CLEARLY FOR BAKING FRESH BIALYS.
REALLY THIN BAGELS!
HUH?
OH...
ALIENS LOVE BIALYS.
YO! I FIGURED IT OUT!
IT'S FOR GROOVIN' TO RADICAL TUNES!
THERE'S NO WAY YOU CAN LISTEN TO MUSIC WITH THAT!
THAT'S CRAZIER THAN WHAT I SAID!
OOH! YOU KIDS FOUND MY OL' CD PLAYER!
I'VE BEEN LOOKING FOREVER FOR THIS THING!
SO, I GUESS IT'S NOT A MUSIC DEVICE.
NO MUSIC COULD MAKE A GUY MOVE LIKE THAT.
END

"SINGING OUT LOUD"

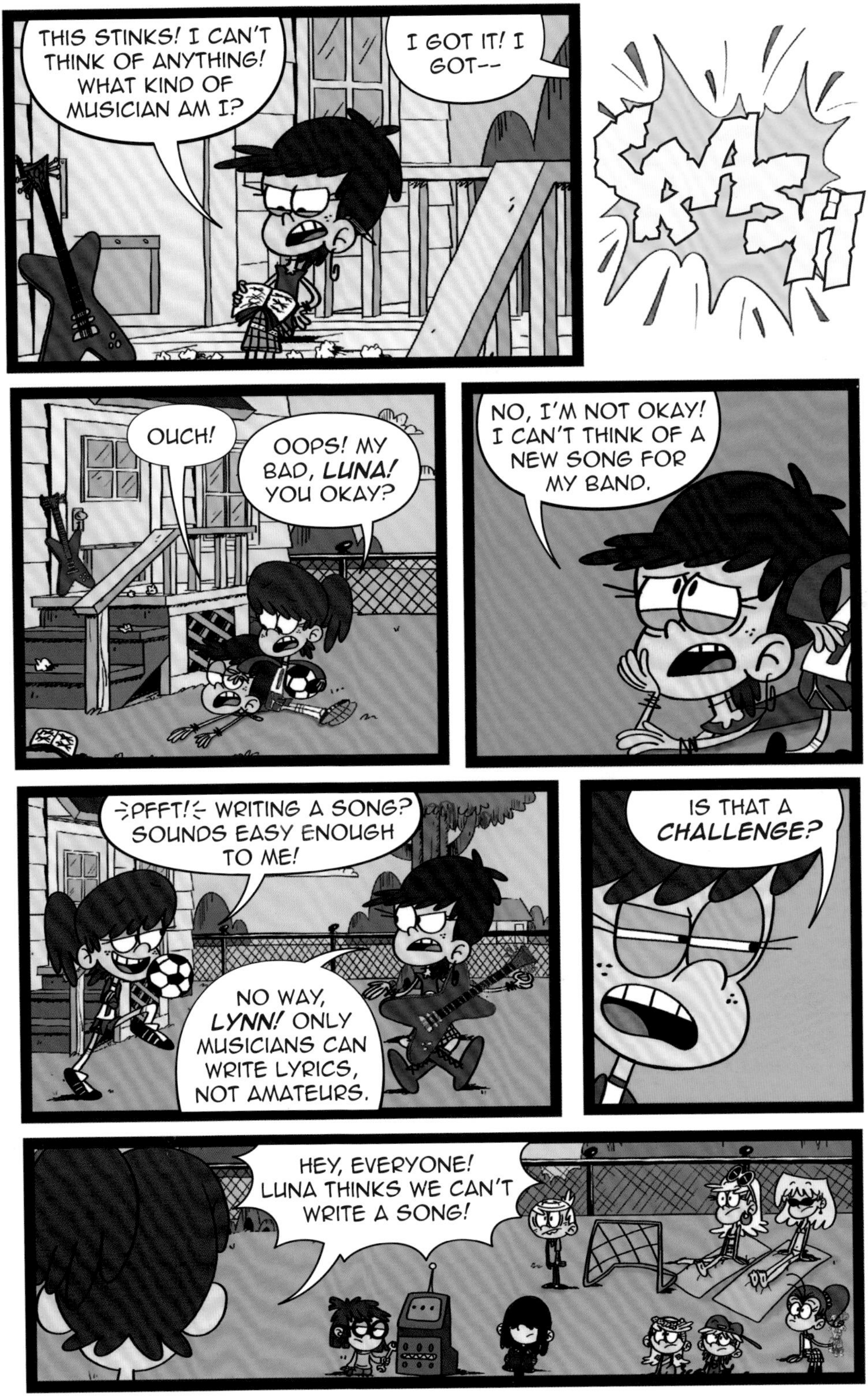

THIS STINKS! I CAN'T THINK OF ANYTHING! WHAT KIND OF MUSICIAN AM I?
I GOT IT! I GOT--
CRASH
OUCH!
OOPS! MY BAD, LUNA! YOU OKAY?
NO, I'M NOT OKAY! I CAN'T THINK OF A NEW SONG FOR MY BAND.
PFFT! WRITING A SONG? SOUNDS EASY ENOUGH TO ME!
NO WAY, LYNN! ONLY MUSICIANS CAN WRITE LYRICS, NOT AMATEURS.
IS THAT A CHALLENGE?
HEY, EVERYONE! LUNA THINKS WE CAN'T WRITE A SONG!

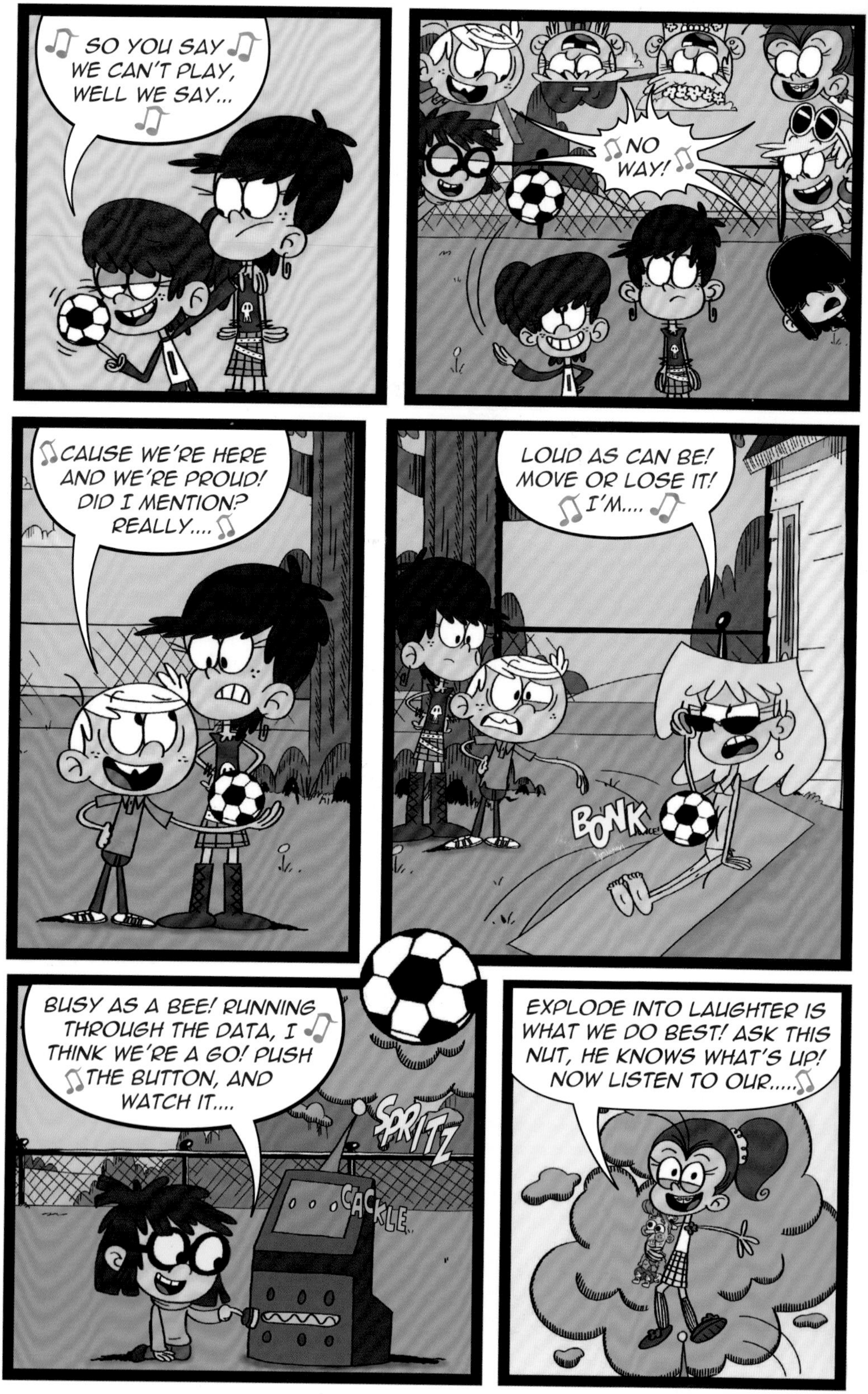
SO YOU SAY WE CAN'T PLAY, WELL WE SAY...
NO WAY!
CAUSE WE'RE HERE AND WE'RE PROUD! DID I MENTION? REALLY....
LOUD AS CAN BE! MOVE OR LOSE IT! I'M....
BONK
BUSY AS A BEE! RUNNING THROUGH THE DATA, I THINK WE'RE A GO! PUSH THE BUTTON, AND WATCH IT....
SPRITZ
CACKLE
EXPLODE INTO LAUGHTER IS WHAT WE DO BEST! ASK THIS NUT, HE KNOWS WHAT'S UP! NOW LISTEN TO OUR.....

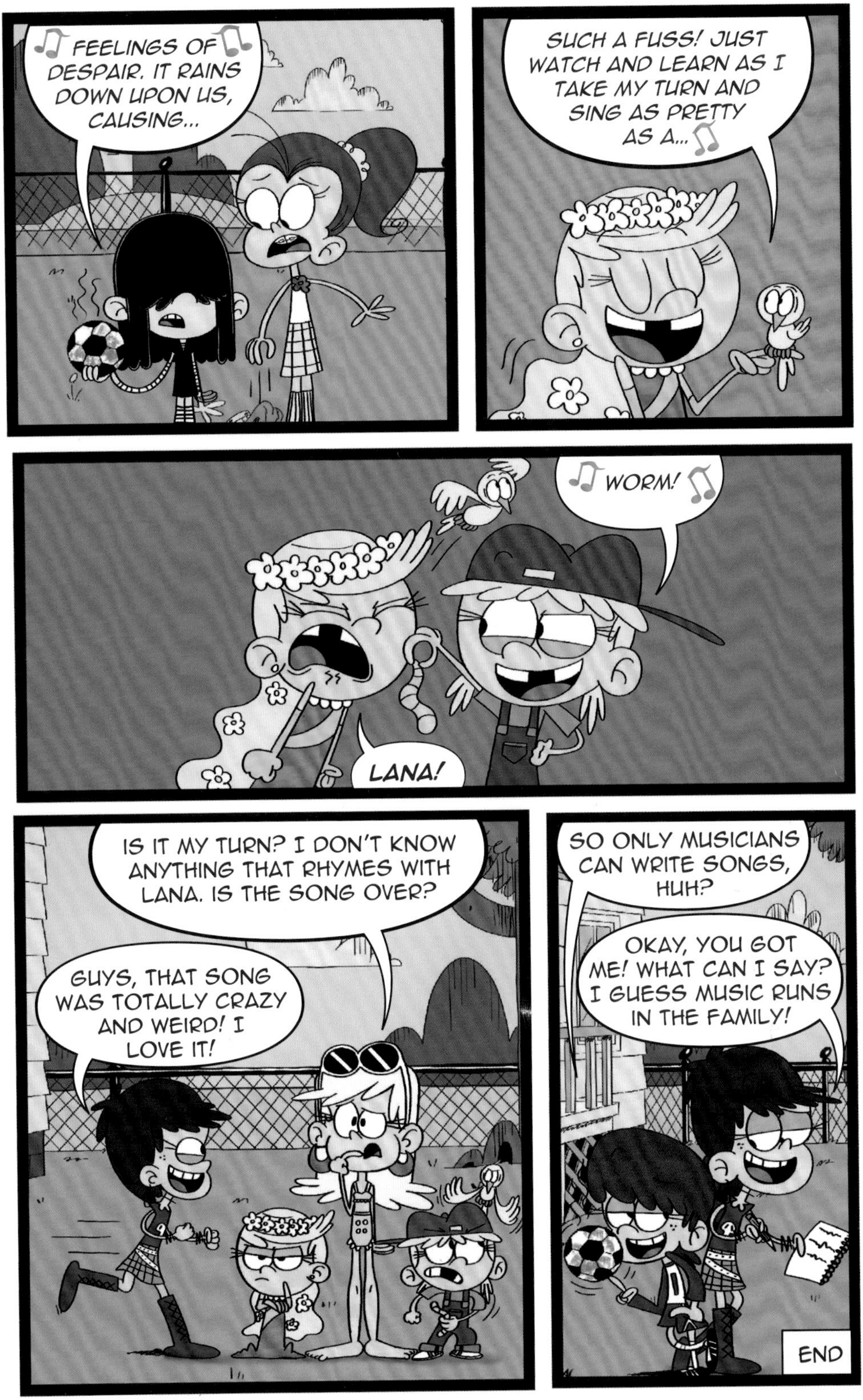
FEELINGS OF DESPAIR. IT RAINS DOWN UPON US, CAUSING...
SUCH A FUSS! JUST WATCH AND LEARN AS I TAKE MY TURN AND SING AS PRETTY AS A...
WORM!
LANA!
IS IT MY TURN? I DON'T KNOW ANYTHING THAT RHYMES WITH LANA. IS THE SONG OVER?
GUYS, THAT SONG WAS TOTALLY CRAZY AND WEIRD! I LOVE IT!
SO ONLY MUSICIANS CAN WRITE SONGS, HUH?
OKAY, YOU GOT ME! WHAT CAN I SAY? I GUESS MUSIC RUNS IN THE FAMILY!
END

"10 SECONDS TO PERFECT"

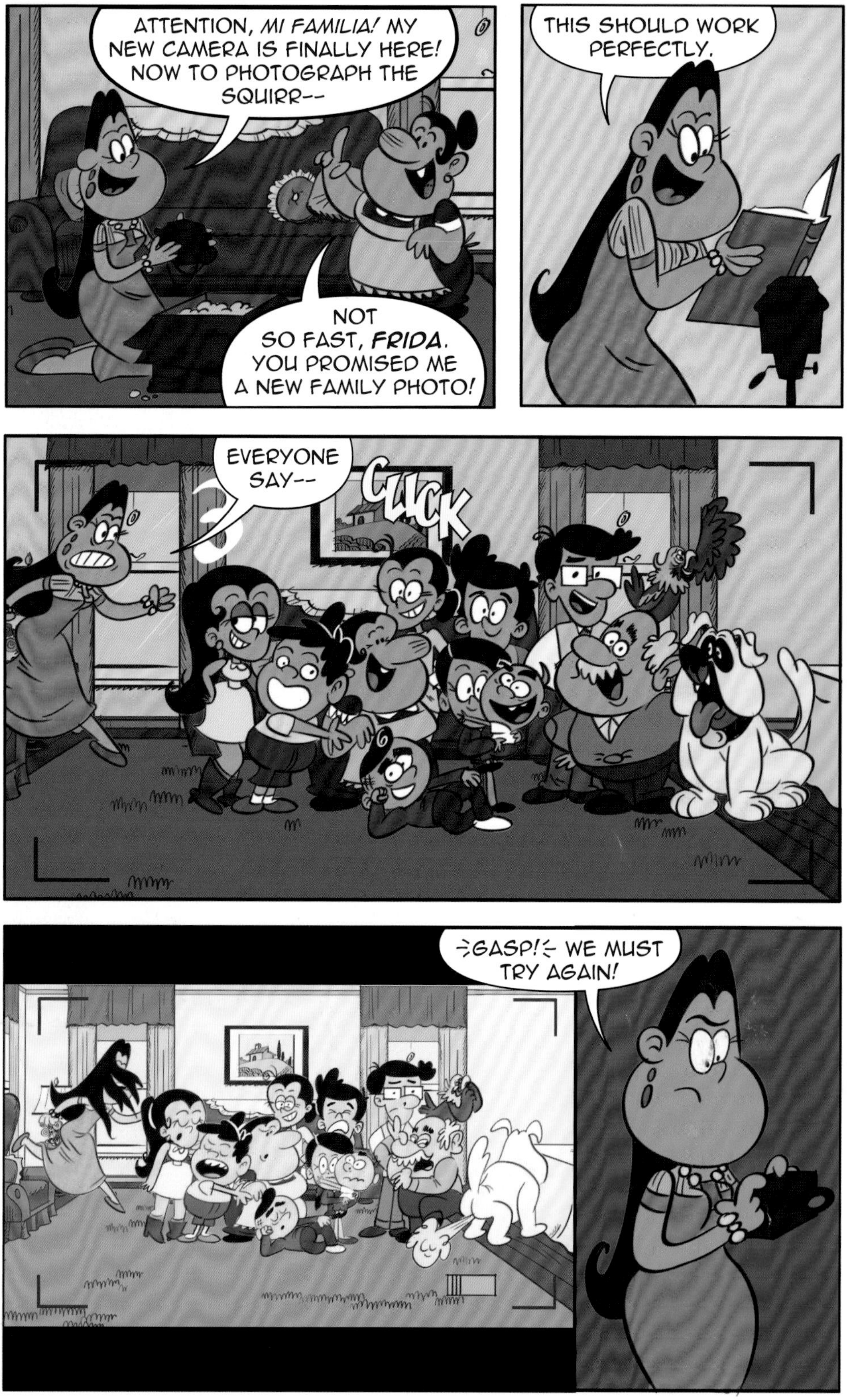
ATTENTION, *MI FAMILIA!* MY NEW CAMERA IS FINALLY HERE! NOW TO PHOTOGRAPH THE SQUIRR--
NOT SO FAST, **FRIDA**. YOU PROMISED ME A NEW FAMILY PHOTO!
THIS SHOULD WORK PERFECTLY.
EVERYONE SAY--
CLICK
GASP! WE MUST TRY AGAIN!

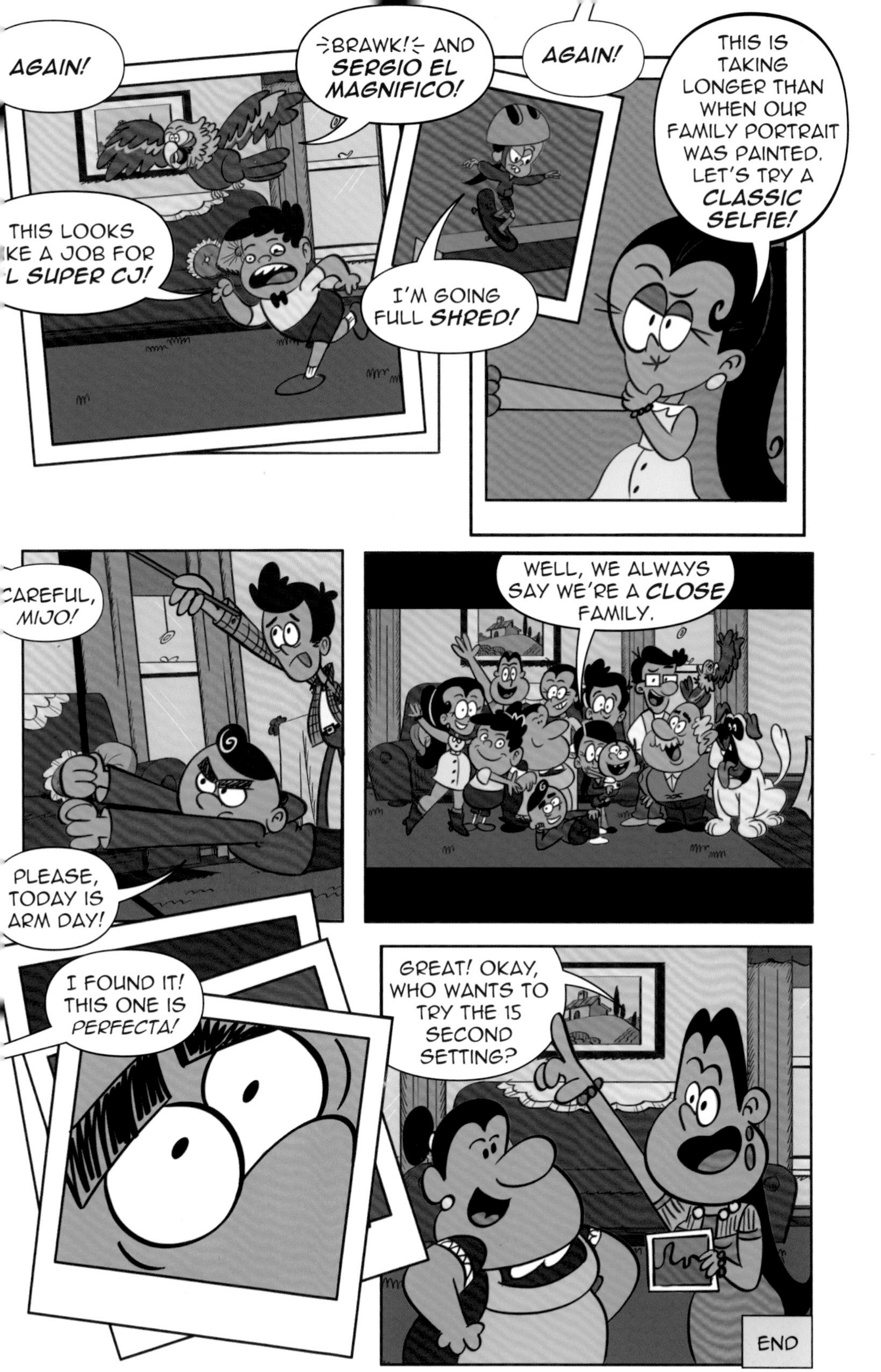
AGAIN!
BRAWK! AND SERGIO EL MAGNIFICO!
AGAIN!
THIS IS TAKING LONGER THAN WHEN OUR FAMILY PORTRAIT WAS PAINTED. LET'S TRY A CLASSIC SELFIE!
THIS LOOKS KE A JOB FOR L SUPER CJ!
I'M GOING FULL SHRED!
CAREFUL, MIJO!
WELL, WE ALWAYS SAY WE'RE A CLOSE FAMILY.
PLEASE, TODAY IS ARM DAY!
I FOUND IT! THIS ONE IS PERFECTA!
GREAT! OKAY, WHO WANTS TO TRY THE 15 SECOND SETTING?
END

"TWINTUITION"

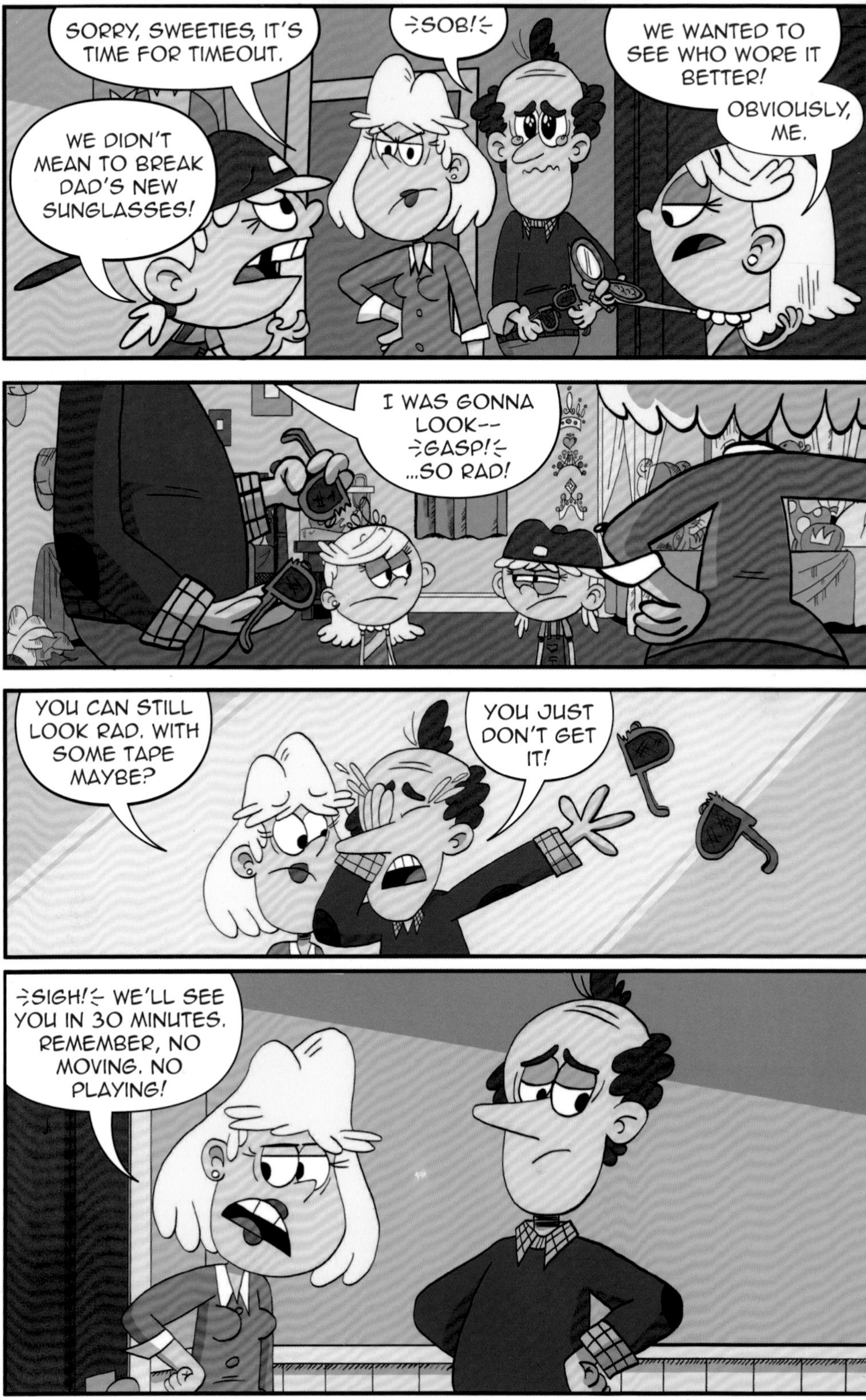
SORRY, SWEETIES, IT'S TIME FOR TIMEOUT.
-SOB!-
WE WANTED TO SEE WHO WORE IT BETTER!
OBVIOUSLY, ME.
WE DIDN'T MEAN TO BREAK DAD'S NEW SUNGLASSES!
I WAS GONNA LOOK-- -GASP!- ...SO RAD!
YOU CAN STILL LOOK RAD. WITH SOME TAPE MAYBE?
YOU JUST DON'T GET IT!
-SIGH!- WE'LL SEE YOU IN 30 MINUTES. REMEMBER, NO MOVING. NO PLAYING!

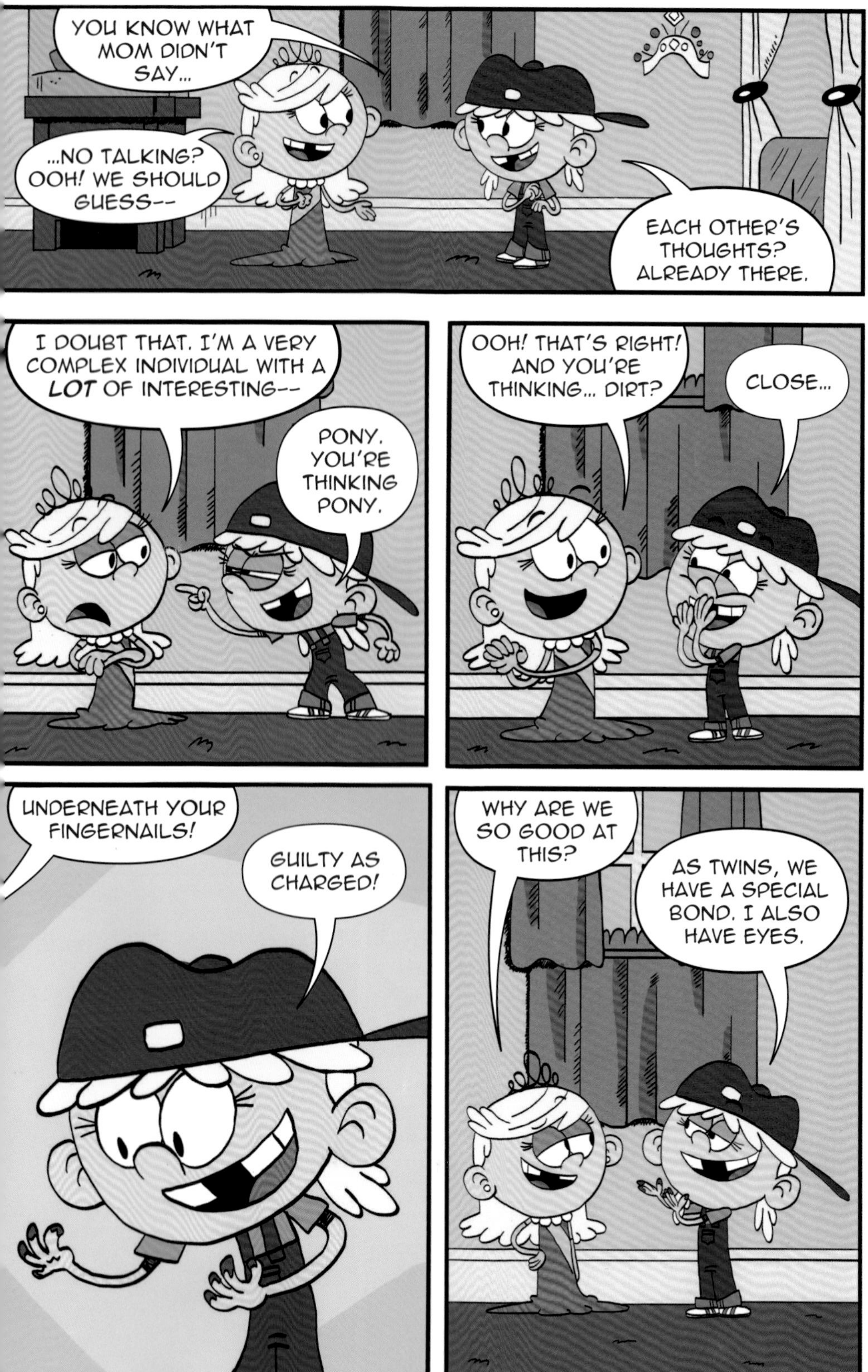
YOU KNOW WHAT MOM DIDN'T SAY...
...NO TALKING? OOH! WE SHOULD GUESS--
EACH OTHER'S THOUGHTS? ALREADY THERE.
I DOUBT THAT. I'M A VERY COMPLEX INDIVIDUAL WITH A LOT OF INTERESTING--
PONY. YOU'RE THINKING PONY.
OOH! THAT'S RIGHT! AND YOU'RE THINKING... DIRT?
CLOSE...
UNDERNEATH YOUR FINGERNAILS!
GUILTY AS CHARGED!
WHY ARE WE SO GOOD AT THIS?
AS TWINS, WE HAVE A SPECIAL BOND. I ALSO HAVE EYES.

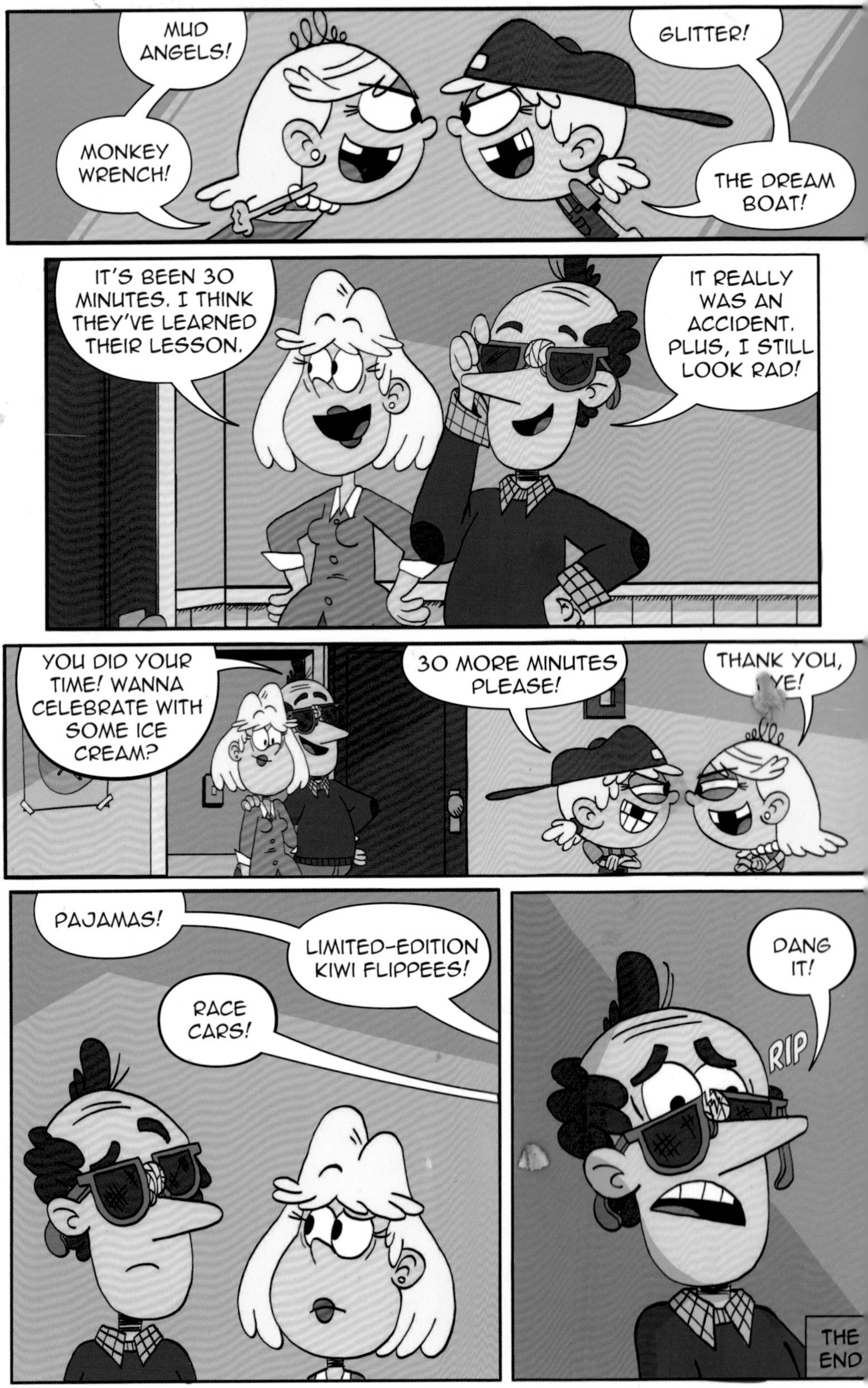
MUD ANGELS!
GLITTER!
MONKEY WRENCH!
THE DREAM BOAT!
IT'S BEEN 30 MINUTES. I THINK THEY'VE LEARNED THEIR LESSON.
IT REALLY WAS AN ACCIDENT. PLUS, I STILL LOOK RAD!
YOU DID YOUR TIME! WANNA CELEBRATE WITH SOME ICE CREAM?
30 MORE MINUTES PLEASE!
THANK YOU,
PAJAMAS!
LIMITED-EDITION KIWI FLIPPEES!
RACE CARS!
DANG IT!
RIP
THE END

"FURIENDLY COMPETITION"

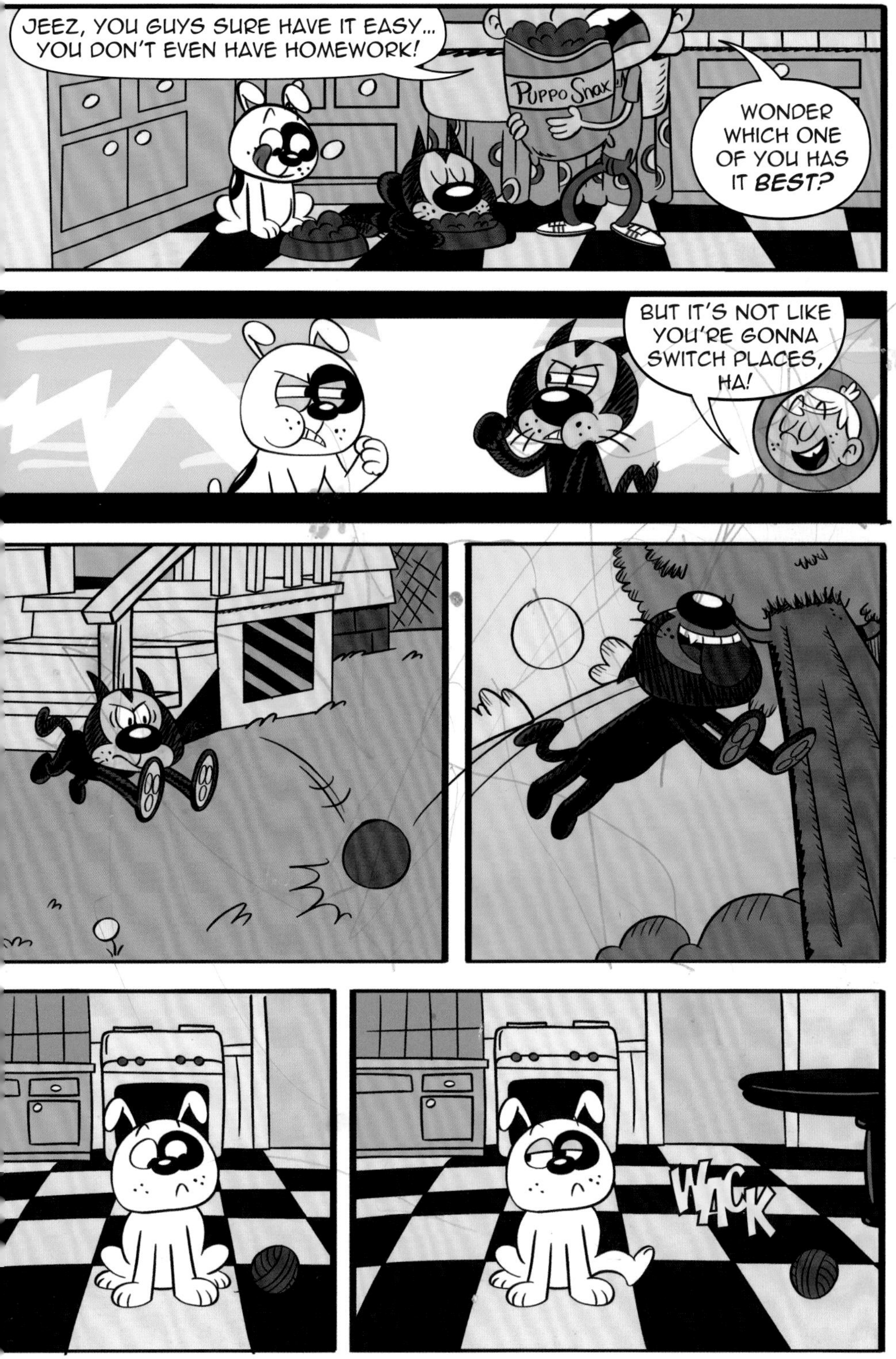

JEEZ, YOU GUYS SURE HAVE IT EASY... YOU DON'T EVEN HAVE HOMEWORK!
PUPPO SNAX
WONDER WHICH ONE OF YOU HAS IT BEST?
BUT IT'S NOT LIKE YOU'RE GONNA SWITCH PLACES, HA!
WACK

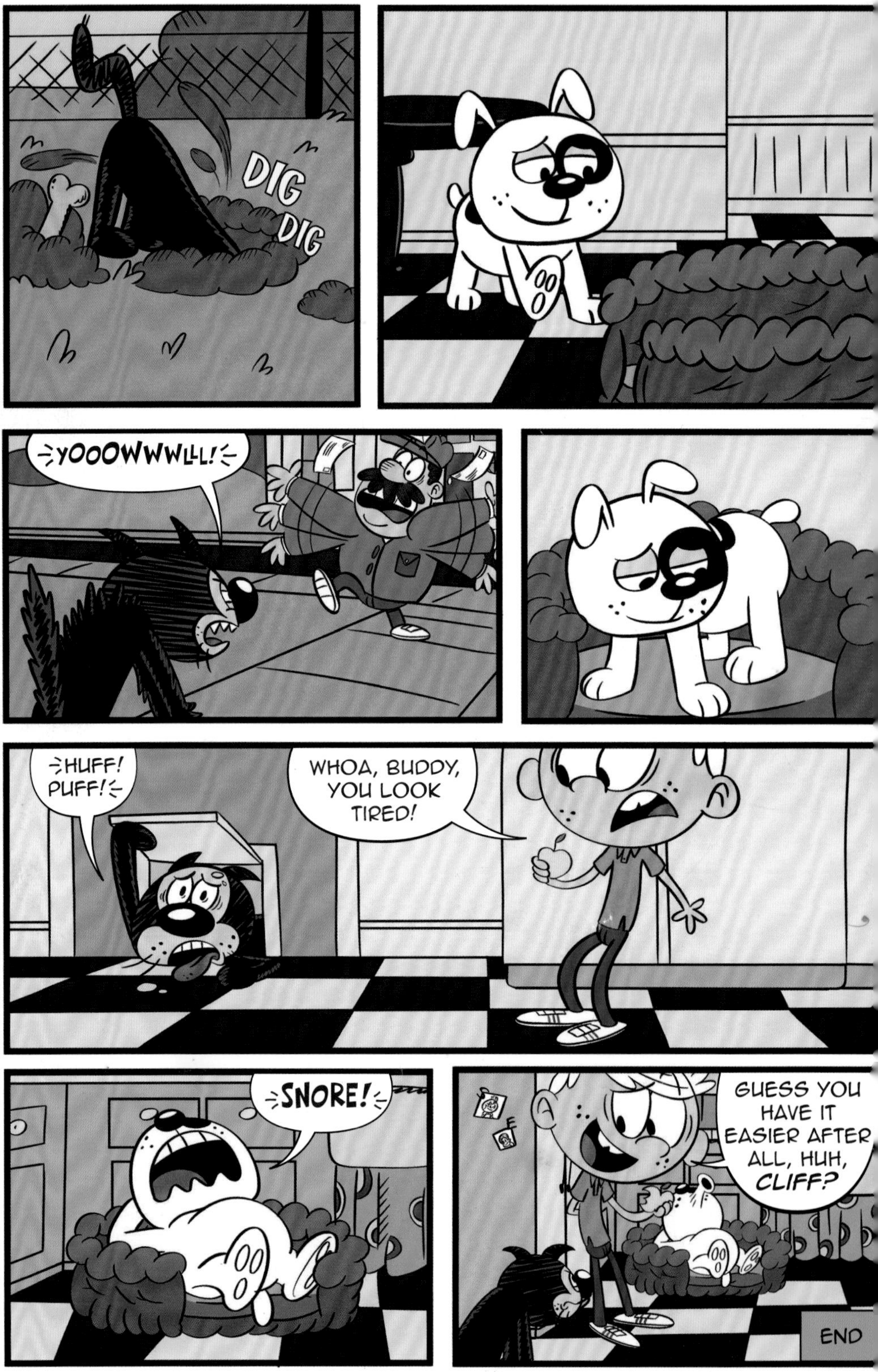
DIG
DIG
YOOOWWLLL!
HUFF! PUFF!
WHOA, BUDDY, YOU LOOK TIRED!
SNORE!
GUESS YOU HAVE IT EASIER AFTER ALL, HUH, CLIFF?
END

"BUGGIN' OUT"

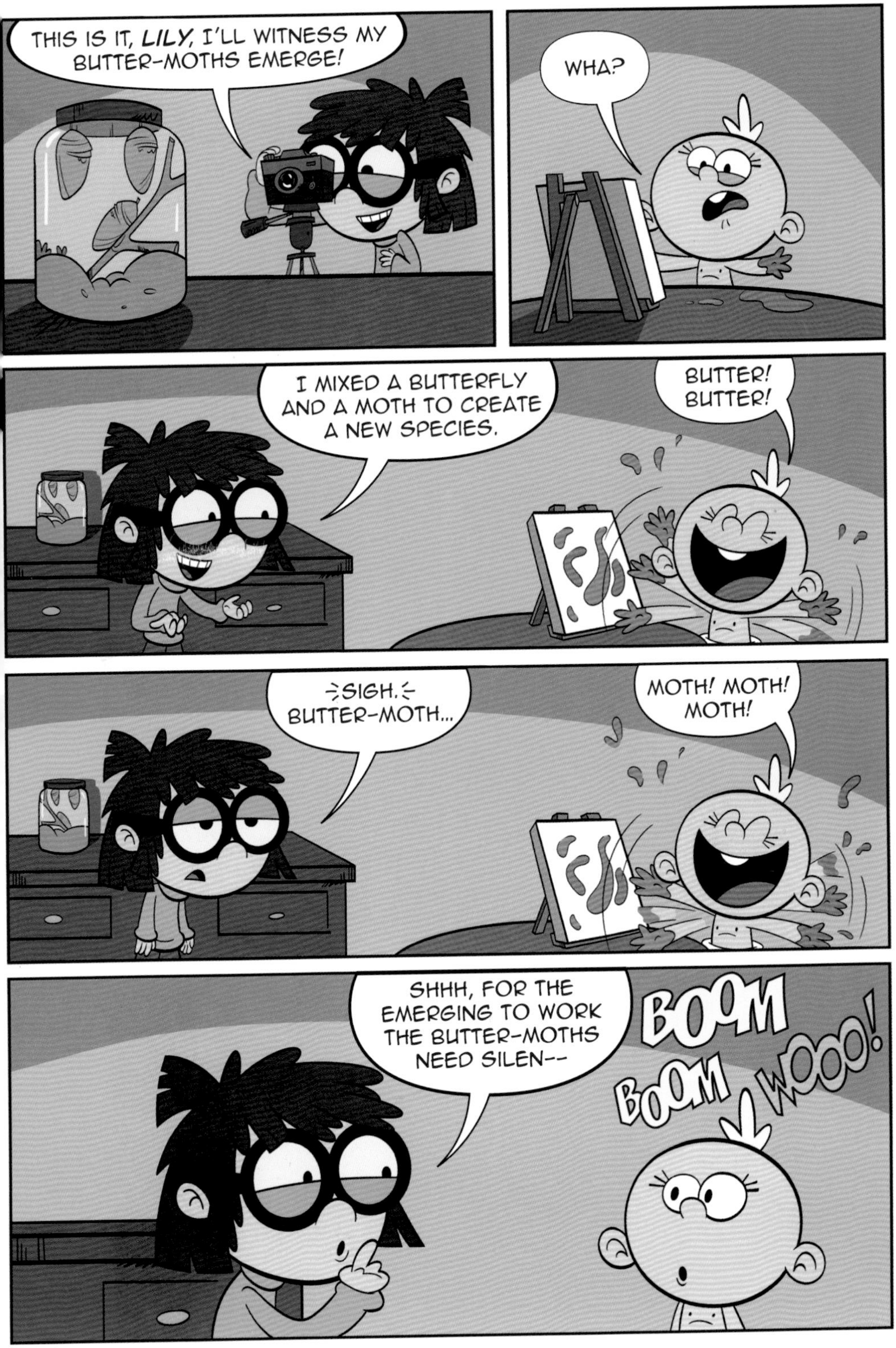

THIS IS IT, *LILY*, I'LL WITNESS MY BUTTER-MOTHS EMERGE!
WHA?
I MIXED A BUTTERFLY AND A MOTH TO CREATE A NEW SPECIES.
BUTTER! BUTTER!
SIGH. BUTTER-MOTH...
MOTH! MOTH! MOTH!
SHHH, FOR THE EMERGING TO WORK THE BUTTER-MOTHS NEED SILEN--
BOOM
BOOM
WOOO!

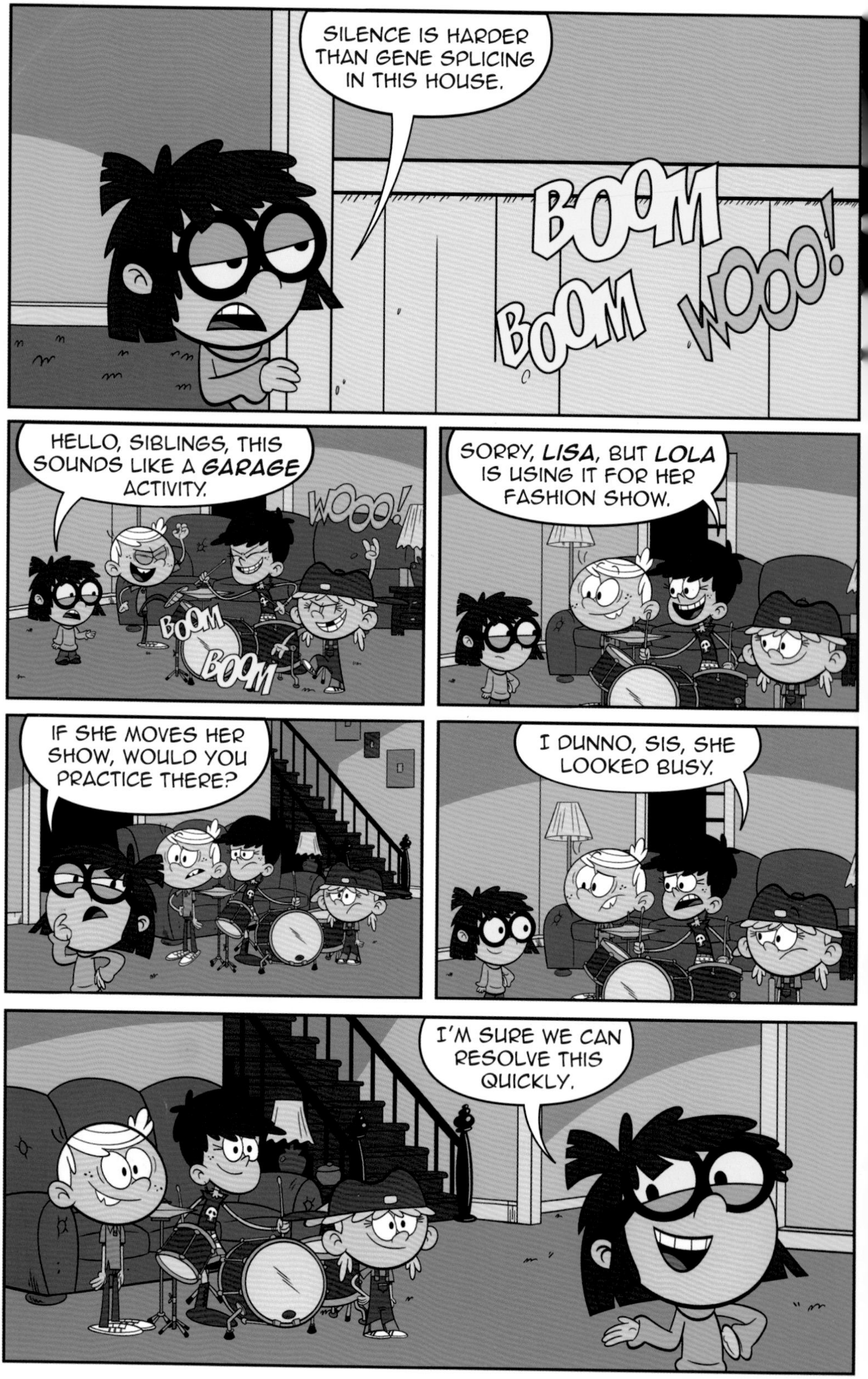
SILENCE IS HARDER THAN GENE SPLICING IN THIS HOUSE.
BOOM
BOOM
WOOO!
HELLO, SIBLINGS, THIS SOUNDS LIKE A GARAGE ACTIVITY.
WOOO!
BOOM
BOOM
SORRY, LISA, BUT LOLA IS USING IT FOR HER FASHION SHOW.
IF SHE MOVES HER SHOW, WOULD YOU PRACTICE THERE?
I DUNNO, SIS, SHE LOOKED BUSY.
I'M SURE WE CAN RESOLVE THIS QUICKLY.

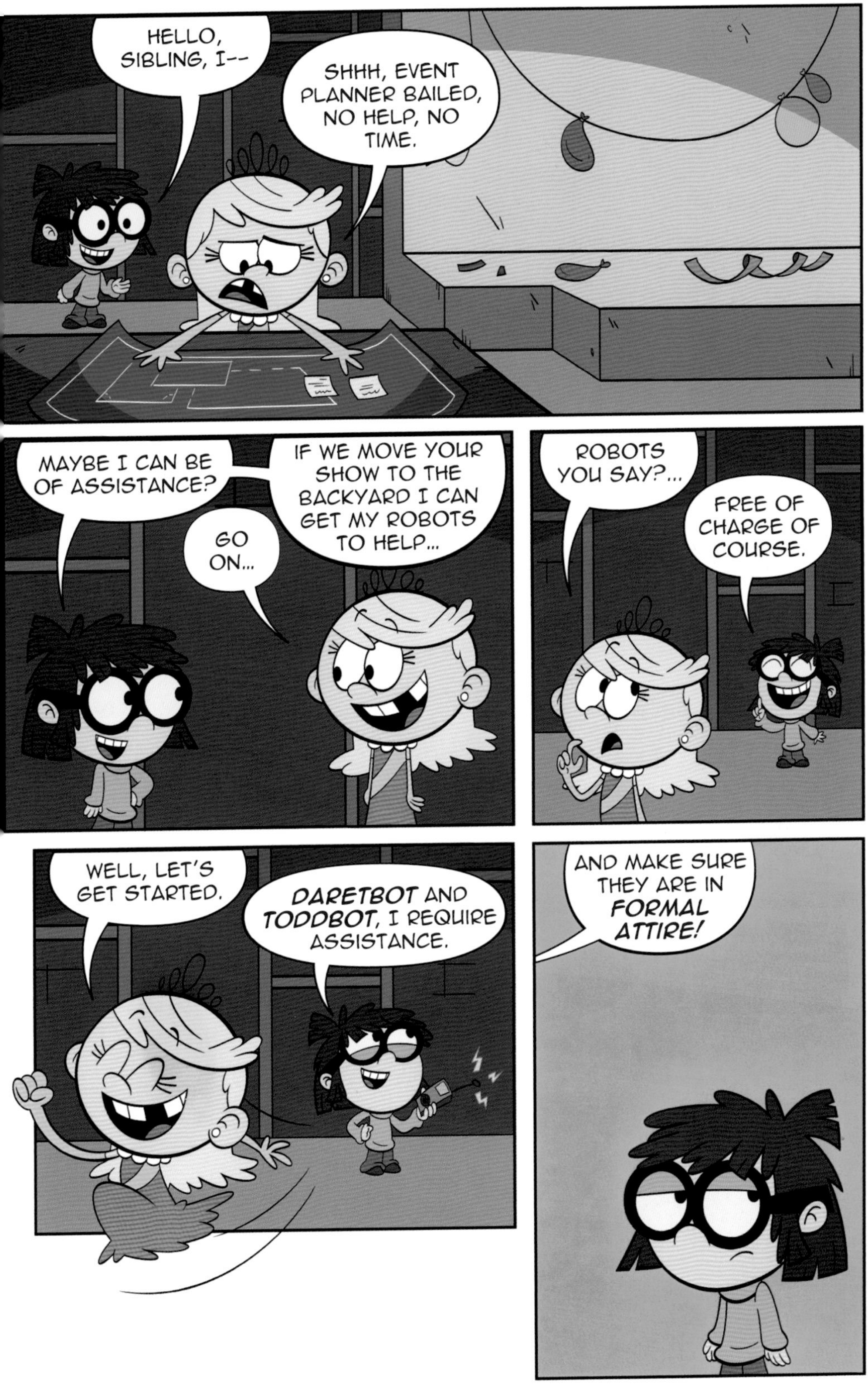
HELLO, SIBLING, I--
SHHH, EVENT PLANNER BAILED, NO HELP, NO TIME.
MAYBE I CAN BE OF ASSISTANCE?
GO ON...
IF WE MOVE YOUR SHOW TO THE BACKYARD I CAN GET MY ROBOTS TO HELP...
ROBOTS YOU SAY?...
FREE OF CHARGE OF COURSE.
WELL, LET'S GET STARTED.
DARETBOT AND TODDBOT, I REQUIRE ASSISTANCE.
AND MAKE SURE THEY ARE IN FORMAL ATTIRE!

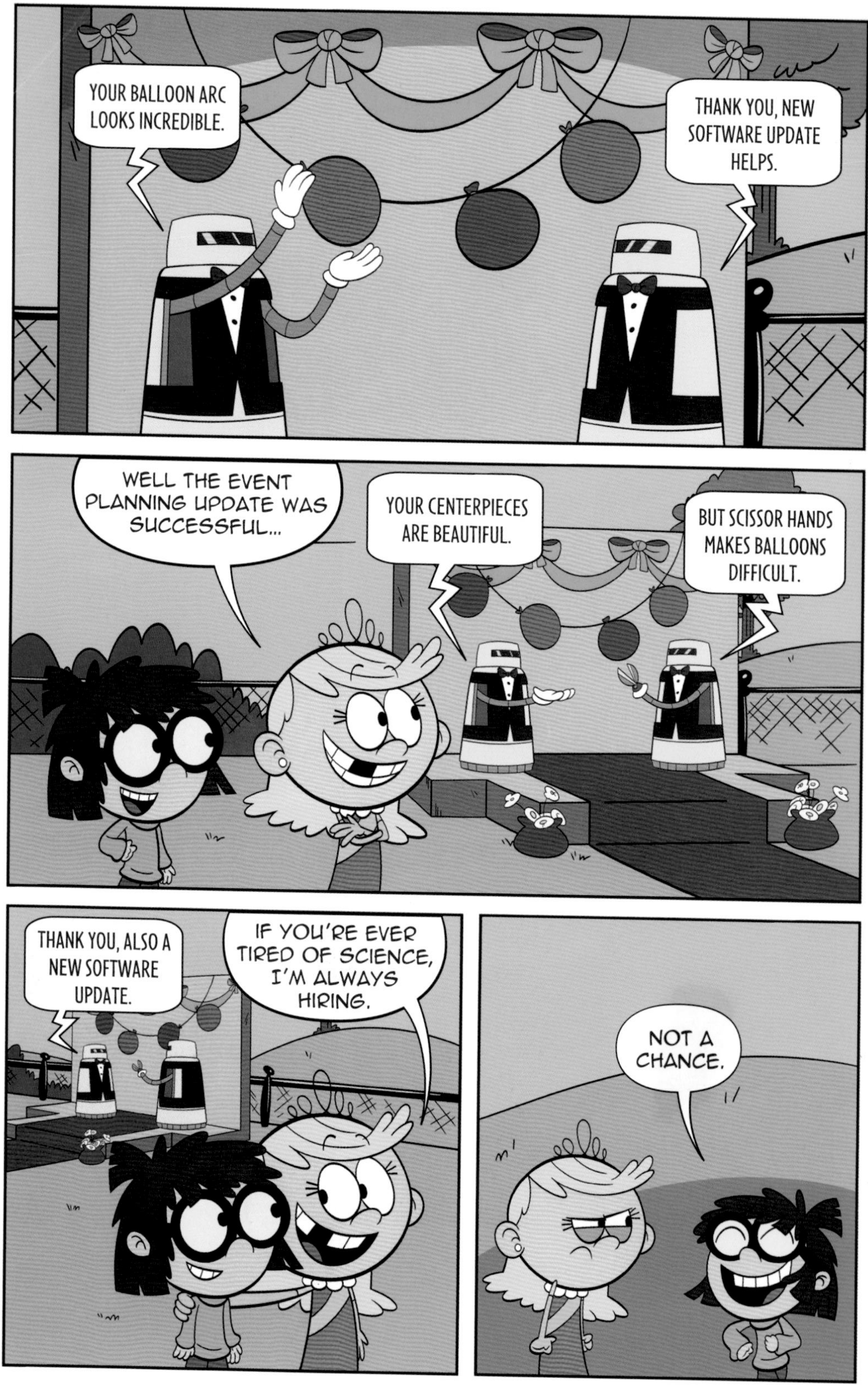
YOUR BALLOON ARC LOOKS INCREDIBLE.
THANK YOU, NEW SOFTWARE UPDATE HELPS.
WELL THE EVENT PLANNING UPDATE WAS SUCCESSFUL...
YOUR CENTERPIECES ARE BEAUTIFUL.
BUT SCISSOR HANDS MAKES BALLOONS DIFFICULT.
THANK YOU, ALSO A NEW SOFTWARE UPDATE.
IF YOU'RE EVER TIRED OF SCIENCE, I'M ALWAYS HIRING.
NOT A CHANCE.

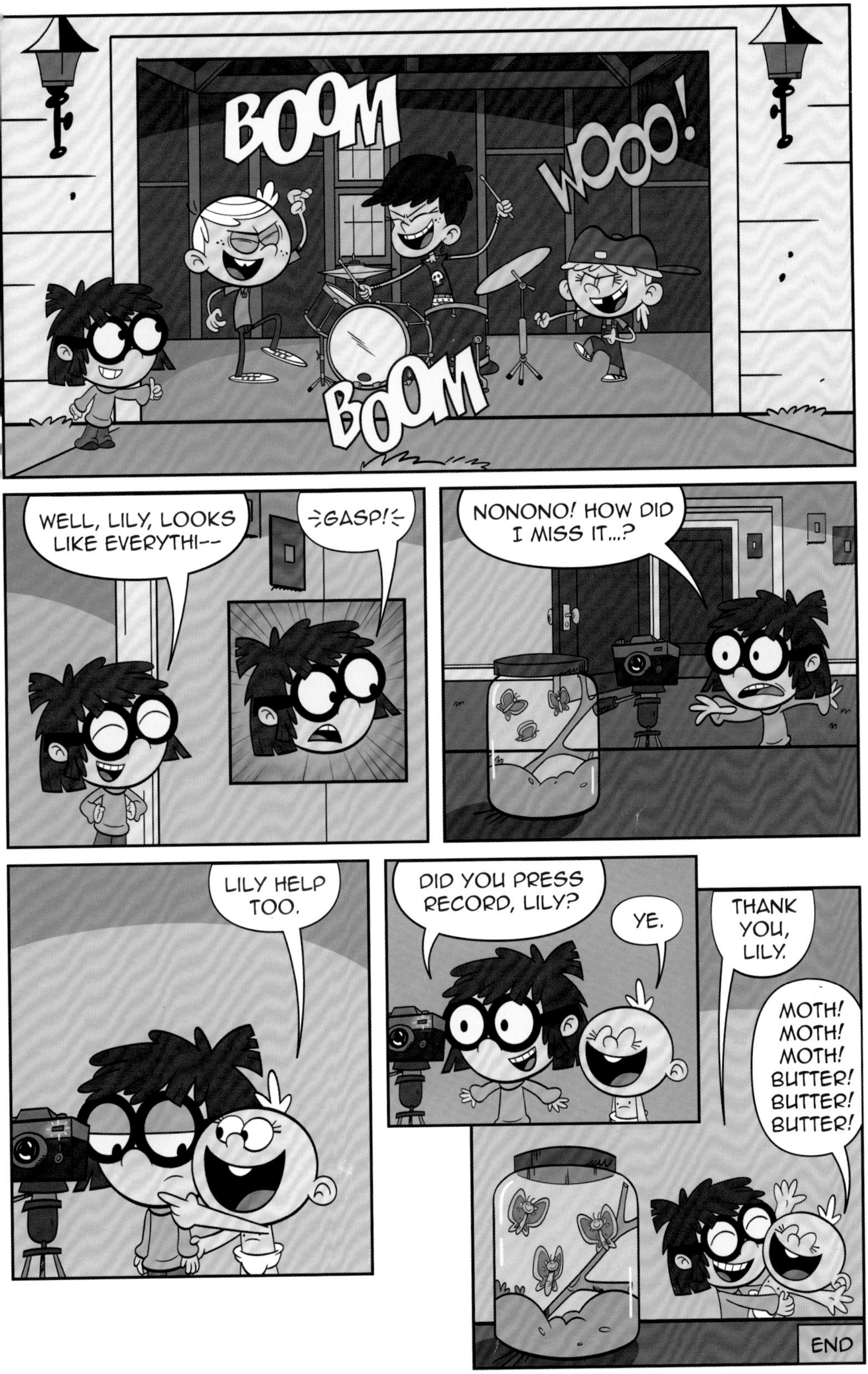
BOOM
WOOO!
BOOM
WELL, LILY, LOOKS LIKE EVERYTHI--
GASP!
NONONO! HOW DID I MISS IT...?
LILY HELP TOO.
DID YOU PRESS RECORD, LILY?
YE.
THANK YOU, LILY.
MOTH! MOTH! MOTH! BUTTER! BUTTER! BUTTER!
END

"SALE FAIL"

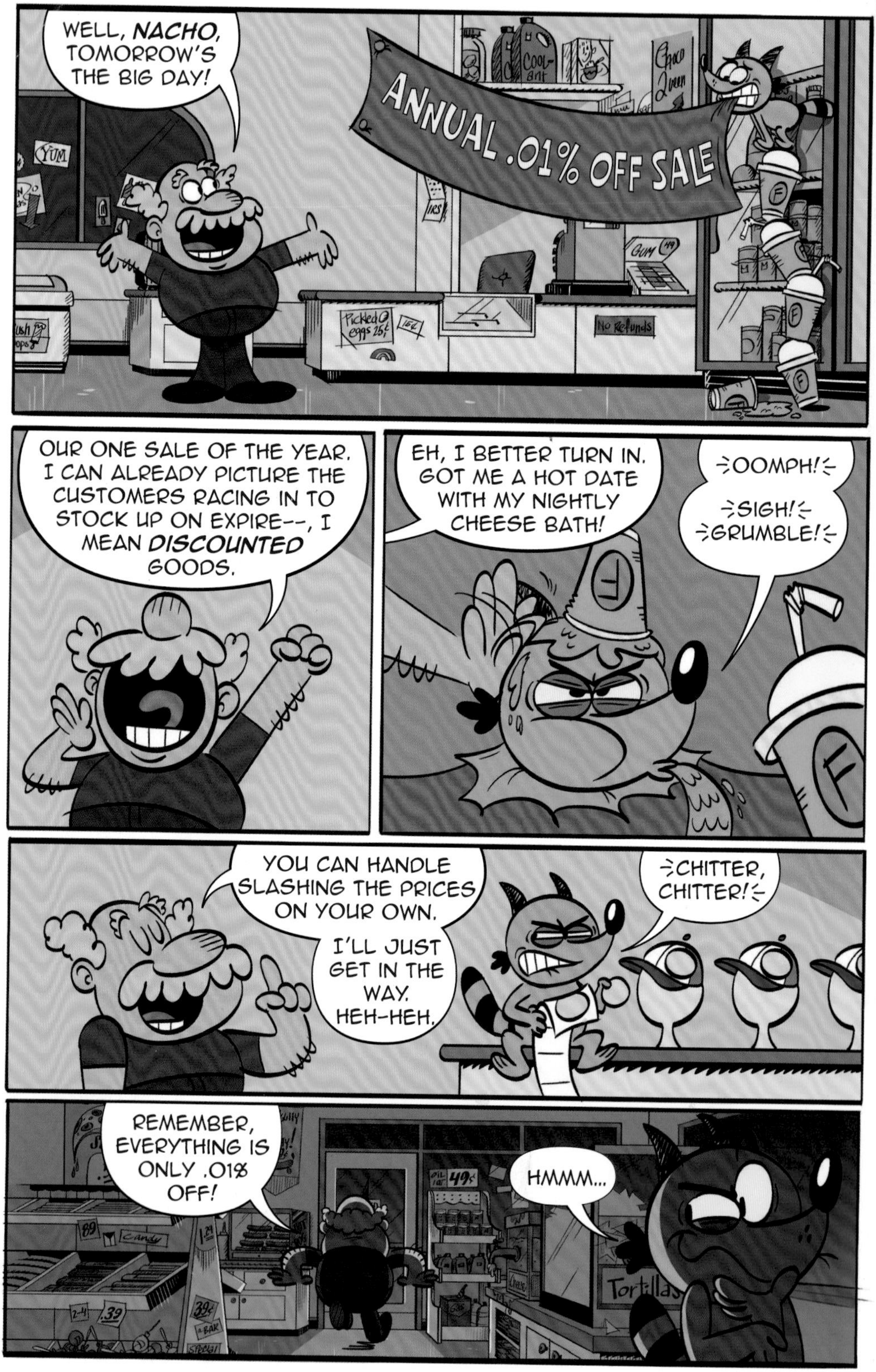

WELL, NACHO, TOMORROW'S THE BIG DAY!
ANNUAL .01% OFF SALE
OUR ONE SALE OF THE YEAR. I CAN ALREADY PICTURE THE CUSTOMERS RACING IN TO STOCK UP ON EXPIRE--, I MEAN DISCOUNTED GOODS.
EH, I BETTER TURN IN. GOT ME A HOT DATE WITH MY NIGHTLY CHEESE BATH!
OOMPH!
SIGH! GRUMBLE!
YOU CAN HANDLE SLASHING THE PRICES ON YOUR OWN.
I'LL JUST GET IN THE WAY. HEH-HEH.
CHITTER, CHITTER!
REMEMBER, EVERYTHING IS ONLY .01% OFF!
HMMM...

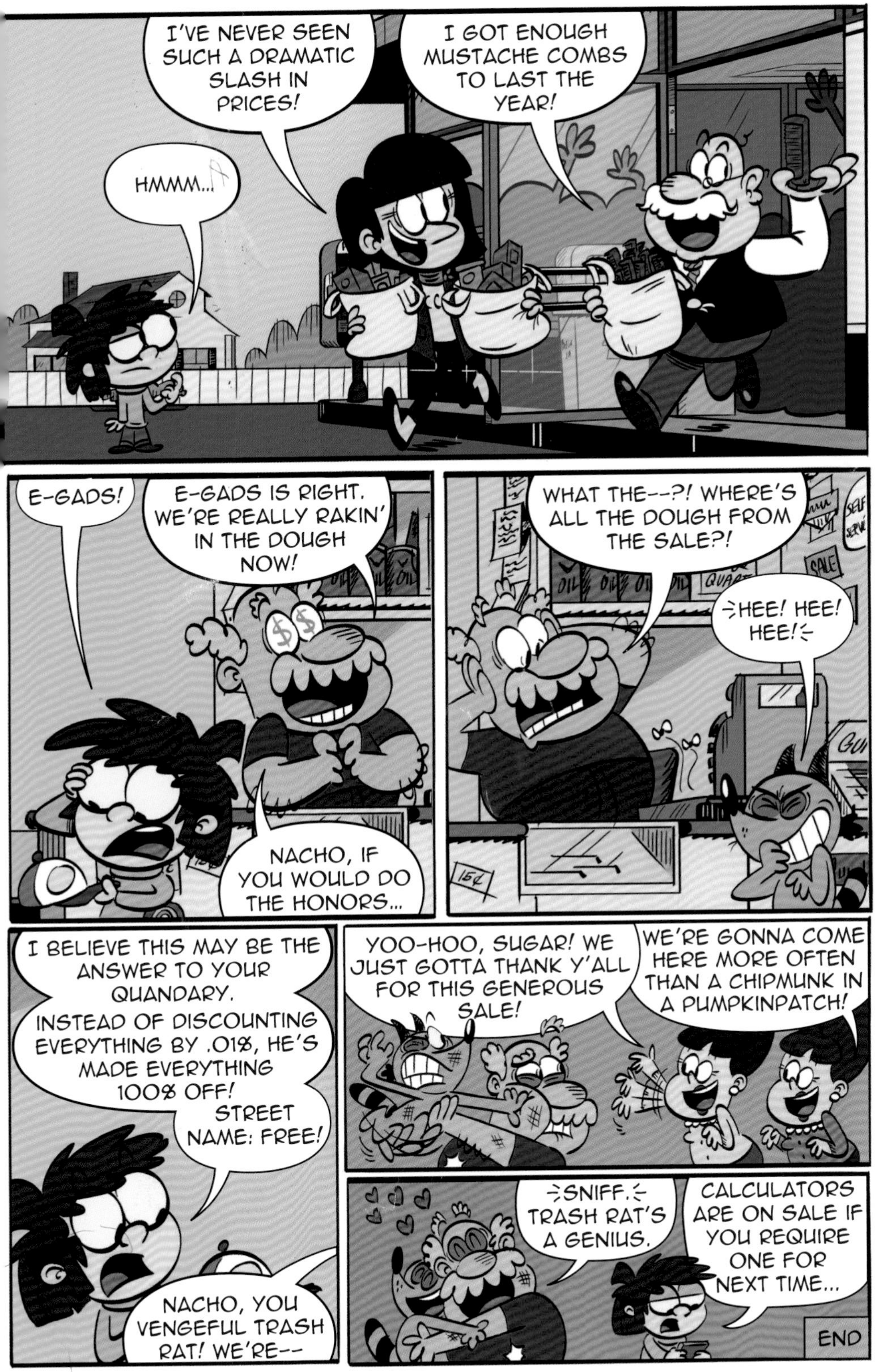

I'VE NEVER SEEN SUCH A DRAMATIC SLASH IN PRICES!
I GOT ENOUGH MUSTACHE COMBS TO LAST THE YEAR!
HMMM...
E-GADS!
E-GADS IS RIGHT. WE'RE REALLY RAKIN' IN THE DOUGH NOW!
NACHO, IF YOU WOULD DO THE HONORS...
WHAT THE--?! WHERE'S ALL THE DOUGH FROM THE SALE?!
HEE! HEE! HEE!
I BELIEVE THIS MAY BE THE ANSWER TO YOUR QUANDARY.
INSTEAD OF DISCOUNTING EVERYTHING BY .01%, HE'S MADE EVERYTHING 100% OFF!
STREET NAME: FREE!
NACHO, YOU VENGEFUL TRASH RAT! WE'RE--
YOO-HOO, SUGAR! WE JUST GOTTA THANK Y'ALL FOR THIS GENEROUS SALE!
WE'RE GONNA COME HERE MORE OFTEN THAN A CHIPMUNK IN A PUMPKINPATCH!
SNIFF. TRASH RAT'S A GENIUS.
CALCULATORS ARE ON SALE IF YOU REQUIRE ONE FOR NEXT TIME...
END

WATCH OUT FOR PAPERCUTZ

Welcome to the fourteenth family-friendly THE LOUD HOUSE graphic novel "Guessing Games," from guess who? That's right, Papercutz, those lucky guessers dedicated to publishing great graphic novels for all ages. I'm Jim Salicrup, Editor-in-Chief and Ultimate Second-Guesser. Guess this is where I tell you about an exciting new special graphic novel featuring the stars of THE LOUD HOUSE. Can you guess what it's called?

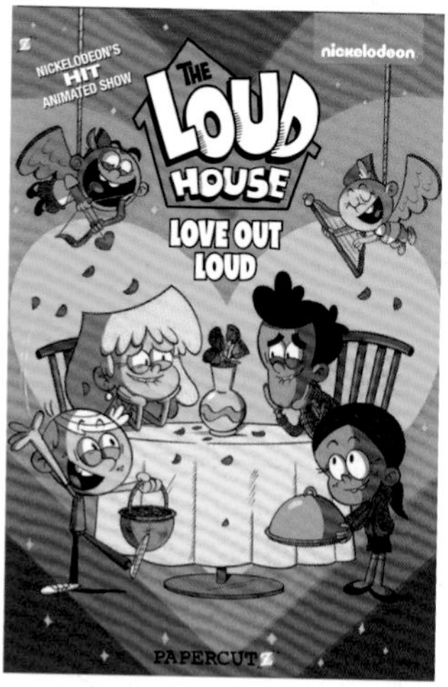
NICKELODEON'S HIT ANIMATED SHOW
nickelodeon
THE LOUD HOUSE
LOVE OUT LOUD
PAPERCUTZ

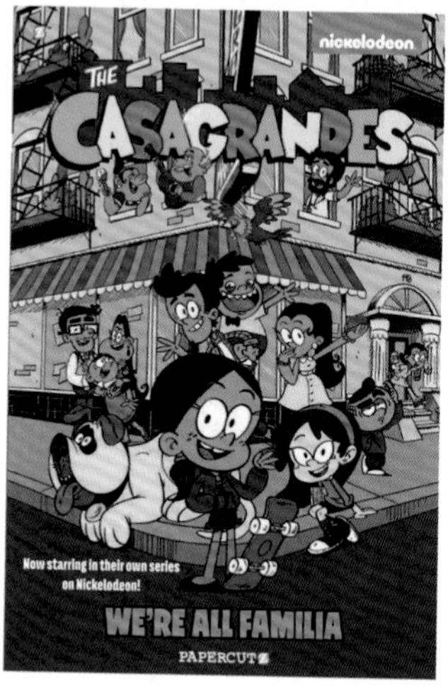
nickelodeon
THE CASAGRANDES
Now starring in their own series on Nickelodeon!
WE'RE ALL FAMILIA
PAPERCUTZ

Give up? Well, how about if I give you a clue? The initials are LOL. Nope, it's not Laugh Out Loud, although that's a good guess. And no, it's not Loud Out Laugh! That would be silly. And it's not Lincoln Or Lily, or Lisa Or Lana, or Lola Or Lucy, or Lynn, Or Luan, or Luna Or Leni, or Lori Or Lincoln ... Okay, I'll give you one more clue. It's something the Loud family has in abundance. That's it! You guessed it! Love Out Loud is the title of the newest, most romantic special edition of THE LOUD HOUSE yet! But don't worry. THE LOUD HOUSE isn't about to go all mushy on you! There will still be plenty of laughs in THE LOUD HOUSE style that we all know and... love! You can even see what we're talking about in the special preview starting on page 62. You'll love it!

But if you're the impatient type and really can't wait another second for the Love Out Loud Special, you could always get more of THE LOUD HOUSE by watching the hit show on Nickelodeon or picking up previous volumes and SPECIALS and 3 IN 1 editions of THE LOUD HOUSE graphic novels. You could even pick up the first volume of THE CASAGRANDES graphic novels. Now, I hope you're not getting the impression that I'm trying to sell you something! The good news is that most Papercutz graphic novels, including THE LOUD HOUSE and THE CASAGRANDES are available at your local library. Of course, if you want to build your very own library of THE LOUD HOUSE and THE CASAGRANDES graphic novels, I'm certainly not going to try to stop you!

I guess I could also tell you what's coming up in THE LOUD HOUSE #15, but in the spirit of the title of this volume of THE LOUD HOUSE, it might be more fun to keep you guessing! Rest assured that there will be lots of stories featuring many of your favorite characters from THE LOUD HOUSE. One of the best things about being an editor at Papercutz is that you get to see stories from THE LOUD HOUSE comics before the graphic novels are even printed! So, while I'm bursting at the seams to tell you about all the stories we've got lined up for THE LOUD HOUSE #15, I'm not going to! (THE LOUD HOUSE editor, Jeff Whitman, snarkily just said "That's not why Jim's seams are bursting," but I'll ignore that.) You'll just have to wait and see. I promise you, it'll be worth the wait!

Thanks, Jim

STAY IN TOUCH!

EMAIL:	salicrup@papercutz.com
WEB:	papercutz.com
TWITTER:	@papercutzgn
INSTAGRAM:	@papercutzgn
FACEBOOK:	PAPERCUTZGRAPHICNOVELS
FANMAIL:	Papercutz, 160 Broadway, Suite 700, East Wing, New York, NY 10038

Go to papercutz.com and sign up for the free Papercutz e-newsletter!

MORE GREAT GRAPHIC NOVEL SERIES AVAILABLE FROM
PAPERCUTZ™

THE SMURFS TALES

BRINA THE CAT

CAT & CAT

THE SISTERS

ATTACK OF THE STUFF

LOLA'S SUPER CLUB

SCHOOL FOR
EXTRATERRESTRIAL
GIRLS

GERONIMO STILTON
REPORTER

THE MYTHICS

GUMBY

MELOWY

BLUEBEARD

GILLBERT

ASTERIX

FUZZY BASEBALL

THE CASAGRANDES

THE LOUD HOUSE

ASTRO MOUSE AND
LIGHT BULB

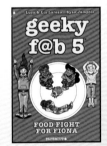

GEEKY F@B 5

THE ONLY LIVING GIRL

papercutz.com
Also available where ebooks are sold.

Get ready for date night with THE LOUD HOUSE LOVE OUT LOUD SPECIAL

"OVER THE LINE"

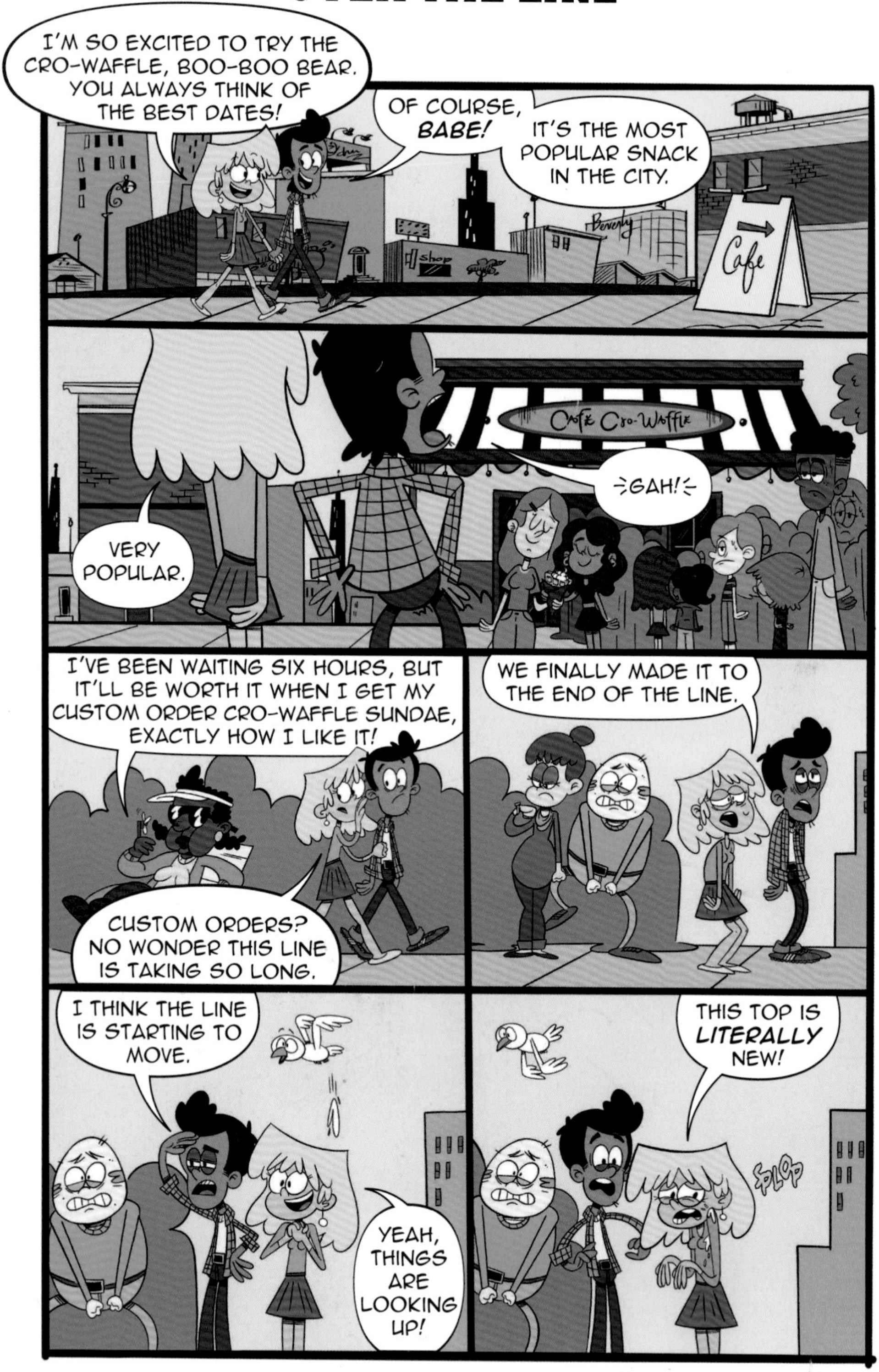
I'M SO EXCITED TO TRY THE CRO-WAFFLE, BOO-BOO BEAR. YOU ALWAYS THINK OF THE BEST DATES!
OF COURSE, *BABE!*
IT'S THE MOST POPULAR SNACK IN THE CITY.
Cafe
shop
Cafe Cro-Waffle
GAH!
VERY POPULAR.
I'VE BEEN WAITING SIX HOURS, BUT IT'LL BE WORTH IT WHEN I GET MY CUSTOM ORDER CRO-WAFFLE SUNDAE, EXACTLY HOW I LIKE IT!
CUSTOM ORDERS? NO WONDER THIS LINE IS TAKING SO LONG.
WE FINALLY MADE IT TO THE END OF THE LINE.
I THINK THE LINE IS STARTING TO MOVE.
YEAH, THINGS ARE LOOKING UP!
THIS TOP IS *LITERALLY* NEW!
SPLOP

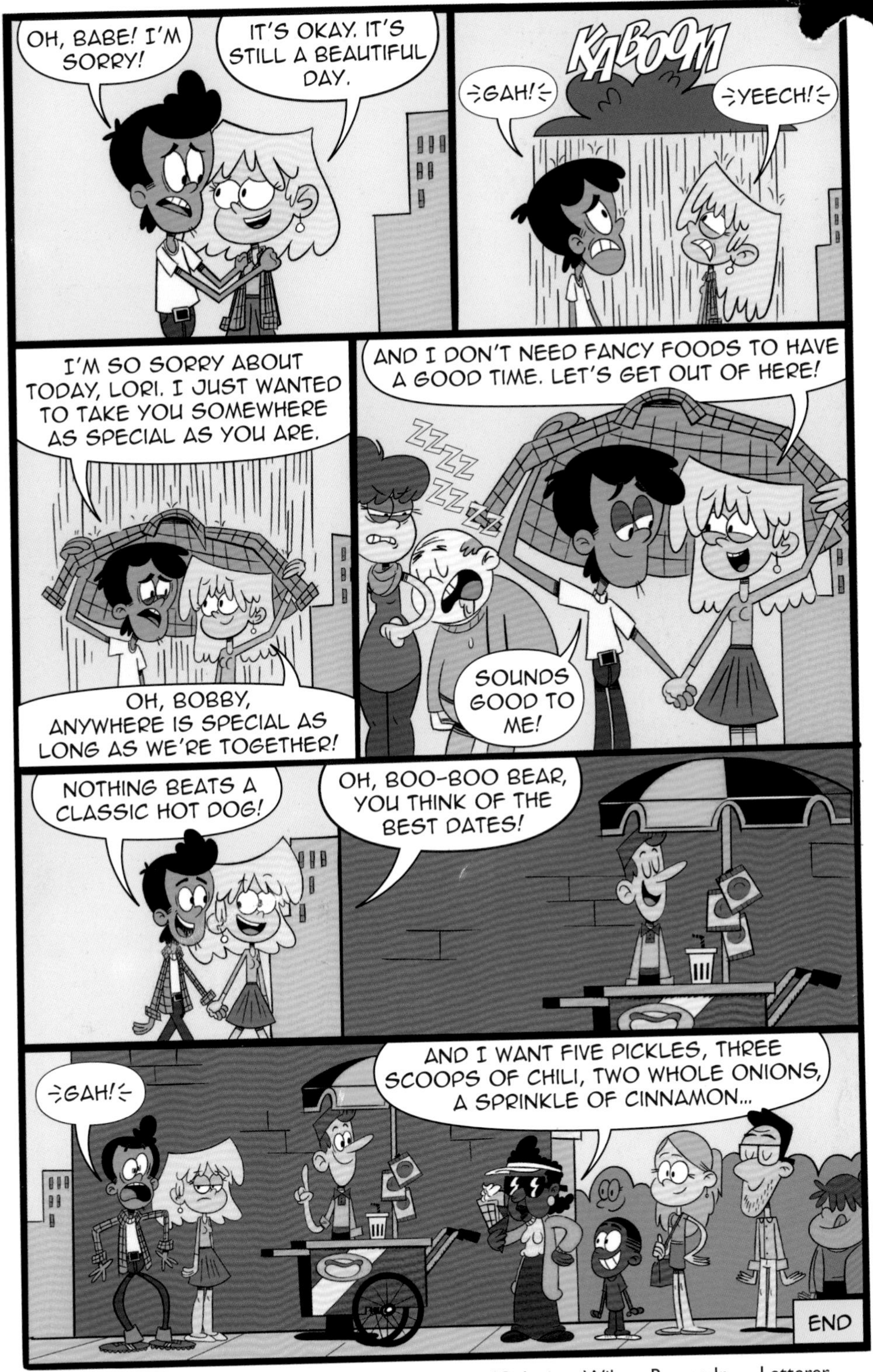
OH, BABE! I'M SORRY!
IT'S OKAY. IT'S STILL A BEAUTIFUL DAY.
KABOOM
GAH!
YEECH!
I'M SO SORRY ABOUT TODAY, LORI. I JUST WANTED TO TAKE YOU SOMEWHERE AS SPECIAL AS YOU ARE.
OH, BOBBY, ANYWHERE IS SPECIAL AS LONG AS WE'RE TOGETHER!
AND I DON'T NEED FANCY FOODS TO HAVE A GOOD TIME. LET'S GET OUT OF HERE!
ZZZZZ
SOUNDS GOOD TO ME!
NOTHING BEATS A CLASSIC HOT DOG!
OH, BOO-BOO BEAR, YOU THINK OF THE BEST DATES!
GAH!
AND I WANT FIVE PICKLES, THREE SCOOPS OF CHILI, TWO WHOLE ONIONS, A SPRINKLE OF CINNAMON...
END

Amanda Fein—Writer • Shannon Parayil —Artist/Colorist • Wilson Ramos Jr — Letterer

THE LOUD HOUSE LOVE OUT LOUD SPECIAL is available wherever books are sold!

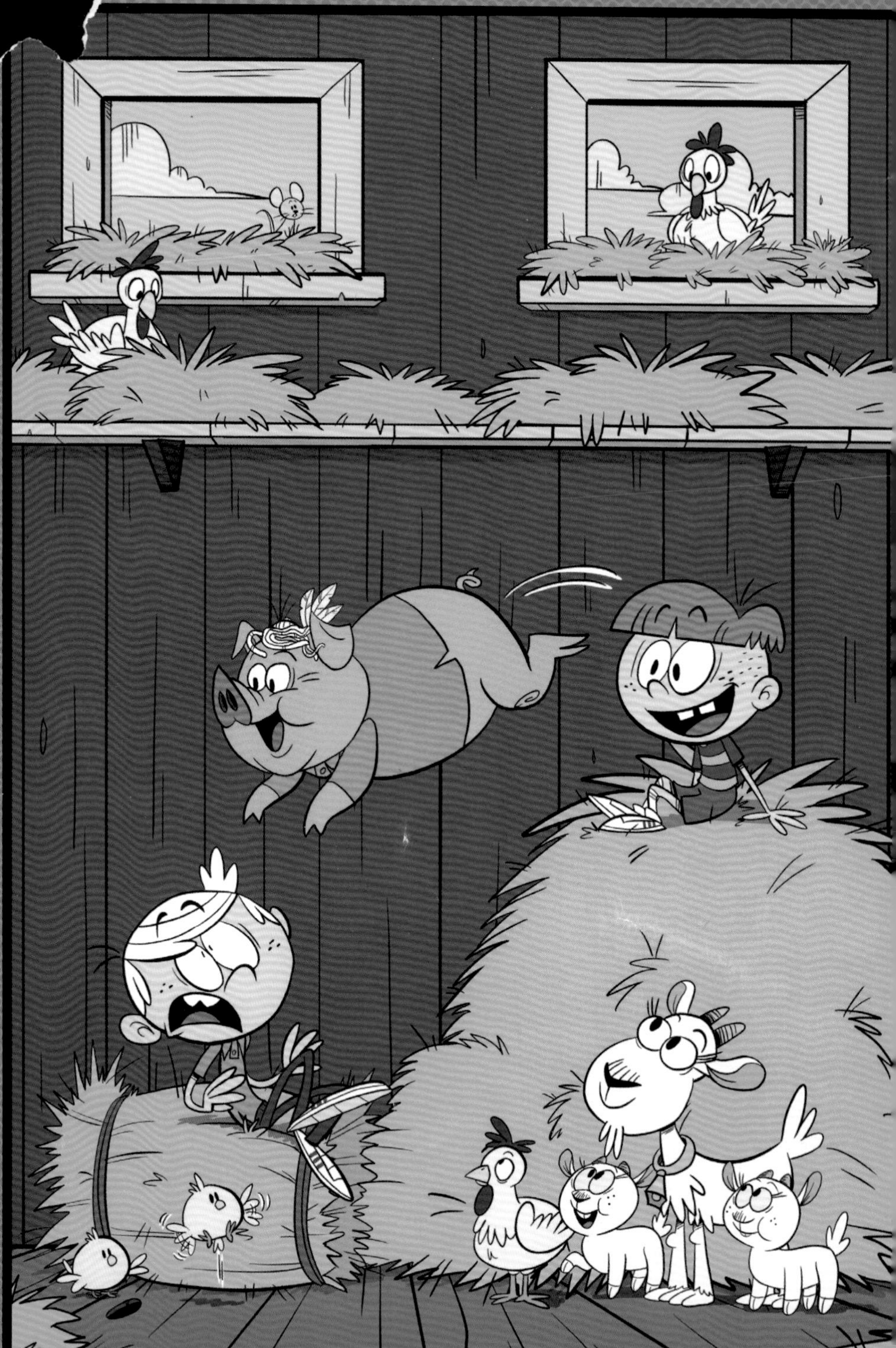

Art by KELSEY WOOLEY